DIL KHOL KE

KIRTI

Made with ♥ on the Notion Press Platform
www.notionpress.com

Love to you dear Kunjal and Ragesh for being my guiding light to write this. You both are the reason that the idea is inked. This one is for you...Dil Khol Ke.

Thank you mummy and daddy for forever having my back. Your anxious wait to hold my book gave me the force to complete it. This is for your blessings...Dil Khol Ke.

Dil se thanks to all the friends and peers for forever sharing with me... Dil Khol Ke.

And to Rahul, for just being there for me. Always...Dil Khol Ke.

Grateful to Almighty for filling my life with loving, caring and trusting people....always Dil Khol Ke.

Cheers to our forever bonding moments...Dil Khol Ke.

Contents

Foreword

The stories in this book are the pieces scattered all around our life. They don't come with any toppings but draw readers into the naivety, tenderness, complexity and emotional realities of girlhood — realities rarely taken seriously, yet regularly lived and felt.

These pages carry moments of courage disguised as ordinary days. Moments of heartbreak hidden behind laughter. Moments of love, rebellion, insecurity, discovery, breaking and healing that together make the world of girls.

What makes this collection special is its honesty.

Every story shared carries the world of a girl — a world shaped by expectations, memories, relationships, trust, dreams, and silent struggles. Some stories may remind you of someone you once knew. Others may feel uncomfortably familiar, as though a buried or forgotten part of your own life has suddenly found its voice.

'Dil Khol Ke' is the bond of such moments that invites you to pause and just feel.

Preface

Our lives are a collection of moments. Some pass like ordinary days, forgotten with time. Others stay with us forever — shaping who we become, and changing the way we dream, live, love and trust. This book was born from those unforgettable moments that live in our hearts.

Each chapter opens a window into a different moment in a girl's life.

These are not perfect moments from reel perfect lives. Rather, these explore the naivety, mistakes, confusion, courage, and hope from simple regular lives.

Some moments were written to comfort.

Some to question.

Some to get an answer.

Some simply to remind that no emotion is ever exclusive and stand alone.

Thank you for joining this journey of moments – Dil Khol Ke.

CHAPTER I

#Walking Ghosts

Have you anytime found something hurting or pinning on you heavier than the actual act or incident? Anytime experienced - being surrounded by human clones, devoid of all humane senses?

Kuch aisa jo galat se bhi jyada gehra laga!

On one regular bright sunny day, I was driving to my work during the early afternoon hours. It was middle of the week and as any other city road, the road was relatively busy.

There was a lorry ahead of me.

I kept moving behind it slowly, thinking there could be something ahead. But then I noticed the driver showing some gestures and not giving way despite the road ahead being clear. I ignored, honked and drove past as soon as I managed to get the space.

Within a couple of minutes, the lorry overtook my car from the left, hitting the side mirror of my car. The lorry then stopped a little ahead. I drove and stopped near the lorry. I stepped out and questioned the driver about this behaviour. The driver said this happened because I overtook and went ahead. In that instance some people suddenly appeared.

“While driving big vehicles such things can happen. When you can have a car, you shouldn’t bother about such small things. The driver didn’t do much”, someone in them said.

I told them it’s fine and I can handle it myself.

Instead of leaving, they surrounded me. Sensing that their intentions are to trouble, I decided to note the lorry number and leave.

As I tried to click the photo of lorry number on my phone, someone hit me hard on my head shouting, "you will drive in our area and then would complaint about our person."

He had hit so hard that my hair clip pricked hard in my head and broke. My spectacles also fell down with that impact. And someone immediately stepped on them.

I immediately tried to call the emergency number. But it just kept ringing. While repeatedly redialling, I tried to stop the passersby to help, but none stopped.

One person from the crowd slapped the driver and asked him to leave. Two others kept moving closer to me. I kept moving back. As my hands touched the lorry, I quickly stepped on it and pulled its wiper. The driver reversed and drove away.

It took some force for them to pull the wiper from me. They pushed me around, telling me to respect and listen to men. One of them, biting his lip and staring hard, scratched my face and hands saying that they are big, it's their area and they can do anything.

By now there was a big crowd around me. All strong enough only to point their phones at me.

I again rushed in the middle of the road, hoping to get some help.

I blocked the way of an approaching car. It stopped. It was a big white luxury car with a single digit number on its number plate. The driver in white crisp uniform lowered the glass. He waited for the owners to instruct. I looked at them with hope.

In any other situation, even I would have perceived them differently. But I understoond that time that looks sure can be deceiving. And, this is how they actually were.

In the middle seat was an obese lady in crisp saree with a heavily painted face. She looked at me and glanced back. On the row behind her was a suited man – today I can definitely say was not a gentleman. Keeping a straight face, he signalled the driver to leave. Driver rolled the glass up, turned the car and drove away.

I was stunned. I was staring at the car zooming away.

Before I could even turn, someone pulled me, twisted and squeezed my hand hard to take the phone and car keys I was holding tight. I refused to let the key go. It was piercing hard in my palm. It started bleeding.

I seemed to not feel any pain at that moment. I was overwhelmed with despair and anger. In an instant, I pulled out my sandal from my foot and hit that man with my full force. Still holding and shaking it high in my hand, I shouted at him to stay away or I will hit more.

There seemed to be a sudden silence. The phones which were pointing at me all through changed directions.

The person I hit, pointed his finger at me. Shaking it, he told me to keep my eyes low. He said, “You have a minute to leave. Don’t raise your eyes. Just go, or else we will burn you now and here.”

I was shaken. I was shocked. I was scared. And I was boiling with anger. But I gathered myself to leave.

As I moved towards my car, a man who rode past on his bike when I was asking for help came back. He said, “I am really sorry. After going, I felt bad for not stopping. I was scared as these people are locals. You also leave fast. If you need help to go to the doctor, I can take you?”

"I managed this alone. I can manage that also. I don't need your help now." I replied sobbing and without looking at him.

I sat in the car. The flood of tears had started before the car started and I drove off.

I held on to myself to not take all this. I decided to file the complaint.

I was directed from one station to another, all far away in different directions after checking the road and junction of the incident.

Phrases I got aplenty! "Oh! You are hurt so much. All those people need strict punishment. Don't leave them."

I lost my patience for being tossed like this to the third place. I now refused to leave without meeting the station in-charge. Finally, they took the complaint.

"Did you think your sandal was a sword?" "Do you think you are 'Jhansi ki rani' and your army is there behind you?" "Stop stopping to question. Learn to ignore." "Duniya aessi hi hai." "Kuch nahi hona. You only have to take care of yourself". "Don't go on that route ever again."

These phrases surrounded me when I reached home-shallowly bruised outside, and deeply wounded inside.

And as the normal norm, nothing happened on this.

But till today I still slow down at that junction. My eyes scout and my mind struggles. Every day I search for those ghosts who didn't stop, and those who didn't step up - more than the men who had all the rights to manhandle.

CHAPTER II

#Hollow Souls

Have you ever experienced being at the crossroad of choosing between hard stand and easy give-in? Ever wondered how some people carry hollow souls inside their bodies?

Jo khud kuch seekhne ke naam se hi boukhla jaate hain, they spoil the beautiful profession of teaching.

I was working as a faculty in a management institute. In that semester I was taking 'market research' for a batch of business management students. Towards the end of the paper, I gave my class a project. The entire batch was divided in groups. Each group had to do market research fulfilling three criteria. First – It should incorporate all the elements covered as part of theory in the class. Second – The area selected for research should be relevant to majority of the class. Third – To ensure fairness for all groups, the names of the group members will be announced after the panel evaluates the research report and announces the winners.

It was an active fortnight. The students were enthusiastically busy. I was excited and happy to see them so deeply engrossed in their projects.

I requested the HOD and couple of senior faculties to be in the evaluating panel. The D Day was here. The panel was sitting. The students started presenting their research reports. The reports were on the issues of the neighbourhood shops near students' PG, hostel facilities, transport and canteen food. The panel was vocally highly appreciative of the depth of the work by students and the applicability of the suggested solutions in the reports.

Then came a report on the classroom experience. The graph in the report showed the HOD and a senior faculty in the panel low on some of the parameters.

All hell broke loose. They both angrily asked to stop the "non-sense" project and left the room.

I was summoned immediately to the staff room.

The moment I entered, the duo shouted on me for giving freedom to students to take up such topics. The HOD banged angrily on my table and asked why I didn't check the findings of the topics before they were presented. They then asked me to share the names of the students in the group who took this topic for research. The HOD warned to initiate disciplinary action against me if I will not do as asked.

"I am sorry for not anticipating this. But I won't share any name. And also, I won't take this tone and pitch," telling this, I darted out of the room.

It seemed to me that I could not walk. I dragged myself, drained by shock, through the corridor. The whole class was waiting anxiously to understand what they did wrong. I told them that their survey result has upset the HOD and the faculty. I told them it should be fine in a day or two. But, right now they are trying hard to get the group members' names to take action against those students.

The students naturally were terrified. I assured them that they don't need to worry as I will not give them any names.

Next day it was a boycott attitude towards me in the staff room. I was surprised seeing how people side the power even when it's at wrong. I was called by the principal. The moment I entered, she said that she has heard what all wrong projects I am giving to students. I need to go to my seniors and now only do as they tell.

I was disheartened and confused about what I did wrong, and what to do now.

Incidently, it was the day of the chairman's visit to the campus. I waited and requested to talk to him when he came. He called me. I briefed him about the issue. He first praised the institute for always caring for the wellbeing of the students and staff. He then expressed surprise at what is there to react so strongly at a simple survey by students. He said, "Rather the reasons behind the poor score should be researched and worked upon, learning and improvement has to be continuous, and we all need to be open for it". He then assured me that there is nothing for students or me to worry as he would take it up and do the needful.

I was happy for being able to gather my courage to talk to him, and was relaxed with his assurance.

Next day I went straight to the class. The students still were worried. They shared that they all were called by the HOD and the faculty, and warned of action if they will not get the names. I assured them that they need not worry. The chairman will now look into it, and all will be fine.

Just then, a message came for me to meet the principal immediately.

I left the class and went to her office. She signalled me to sit. She told sweetly that I am too naive to understand the mal intentions of students for taking up something like teaching quality of faculties. "Such students need to be guided and corrected appropriately". She then kept a paper and pen in front of me and asked to write the names of those students. She said, “don't worry. I am not going to tell outside that you gave these names. We will anyways get the names even if you won't give. Someone from class will surely give us. But, if you will give us, you will prove that you are with us, and not involved with those students."

I tried to explain that survey had nothing inappropriate and she should once see the parameters and report.

She refused to listen. She said, "the names of students, or your resignation on the paper".

I said, "I am definitely very much with you and all the faculties. But I can't leave my students."

She started hurling abuses, commenting negatively on my schooling, my family, my looks – pretty much on everything she could lay her tongue on.

I had never heard in my life what all she said in those few moments. More so, all this coming from a 'sister nun' figure I revered dearly all through my growing years was a shocker. I was so choked that even breathing felt harder. I scribbled my resignation on that paper and left, rivers flowing down my eyes all through the way and day.

Next day the students came to my house. I was pleasantly surprised to know their effort in getting my address. They were feeling responsible for what all happened. They asked me to give their names and come back. They said if I will not give, they themselves will go and give their names.

I knew I could never breathe in a place with such hollow souled and stone headed people.

I told them, "I will get work anywhere. But, experiencing that attitude first hand, I know it will negatively impact your career. You focus only on your career right now, and don't let anything harm it. My resignation will appease their ego and they might not pursue it more with you all."

They left with heavy heart, teary eyes and tongue tied with their limitations.

Their love and wishes I got in abundance, and I cherish that dearly in my heart, forever.

CHAPTER III

#ME Too

Have you ever got the realisation of being subjected to a wrong doing after a long lapse of time?

Kuch aisa, jo baad mein samajh aaya, ki jab hua tha galat tha!

I was about to complete my post-graduation. I was super delighted for being the first student to get a job offer even before writing the final exams. As part of the confirmation process, I had to submit a medical certificate along with other required documents and reports.

Like most families that time, we also had our family physician. On the ground floor of his house, he had a clinic. In the evenings he used to attend patients for few hours there.

For all medical consultations and treatments, the complete extended family too visited him. He had been more like a family member for all of us than just a doctor.

My parents told me to go and get the medical certificate from him.

I went to his clinic, wished him and told him about the certificate.

He said that some basic parameters will have to be checked and ECG will have to be done and attached along with the certificate. He checked my weight and BP and asked me to go inside and wait for the ECG.

I went and sat inside. After some time he came. Pointing at the bed he said, "open your bra and lie down."

I went pale. He said to hurry up and come for ECG. He sat on the stool near the bed and started setting a machine.

Hesitant, I opened my bra button and lied down. He asked me to raise my shirt up. I pulled it up little. He said to pull it up full. I did little more. He said, "Don't worry. ECG has to be done. Close your eyes and relax. I will quickly complete the test."

He pushed my shirt up. I shut my eyes tight. He put few patches with wires below my chest and on my hands.

He then started moving his hand all around my breasts.

My heart was pounding. I could feel myself sweating.

"Stay calm. Just relax. Your report is not coming fine. The readings are not coming good. If you will be calm then only the report will be proper," I heard.

I tried hard to calm myself. But, could feel myself panicking. Feeling nervous I told him that I will come back again for the test.

Pressing harder, he said, "stay calm. Just few minutes and I will complete and give the certificate."

I was trying hard but could feel the tear drops seeping out from the sides.

He said, "Good. Everything is fine. The report has come proper. Nothing to worry. You can come out. I will prepare the report."

I heard him pushing the stool back and leaving. I opened my eyes, quickly pulled my shirt down and got up. I closed my bra and slowly came out.

He gave the certificate and report. I quietly took it and rode back home, all through telling myself that I will never get an ECG done again.

I reached home. My parents checked the certificate and report. I said, "I am not sure why ECG had to be done for this certificate."

My father said, "He is a doctor, not you. He knows what has to be done."

Training, job, marriage, kids - and all things around these- engrossed me for many years.

And then I was prescribed an ECG related to a health check-up.

The anxiety struck me back.

I went inside with the nurse. The nurse completed the ECG and asked me to wait out.

I was confused. I asked, "Is it ECG? Is it completely done?"

The nurse looked at me sternly, gave a blunt yes and left.

That blunt yes was a big blow for me.

The memory of my first ECG turned into a nightmare. I realised then, 'that the first ECG was not an ECG!'

It was the misuse of the naivety. It was the abuse of the trust. It was the harassment.

CHAPTER IV

#Superhero Blooper

Has anytime something made you panic as if the sky is falling? And to stop it you prepare yourself hard like a warrior! And, then you realise it was nothing but a bubble.

I was in my late teens, and so were some of my cousins. My siblings and cousins were a gang. I was mostly outcast. They would always tell that I spill their secrets to my mom and then it reached their moms. So, I was mostly out of their circle.

One day me and my sister were working together in our room. After a long silence she said, "There is something serious I want to tell you. But can't, because you will tell mom."

My big sister umbrella wings opened, and I had to definitely know it.

I promised her that I will not tell anyone. And, it didn't need much effort. She was anxious to tell. My promise gave her the needed nudge and the beans spilled.

One of our cousins was friendly to a girl staying next to his house. He was sad as his friend befriended that girl. Now my sister was sad for our cousin. I asked, "what is there to be so sad in this." She said, "you are not getting it. That boy is not serious about this. It is only 'time pass' till his college starts. The cousin is feeling bad for introducing them to each other. I am feeling bad as the cousin can't do anything."

"It's simple," I said, "He should either tell his friend or that girl. Afterall he is the link in between." My sister said that he can't be bad, as the boy is his good friend.

I was stressed and kept thinking on this for long. Next day I told my sister that I am going to meet that girl and tell her everything.

My sister was angry. "You promised you will not tell anyone. I should have not told you. You will now go and tell the girl. Her parents will know, and then our cousin's mom will know. He will be pulled. He will be upset with me..." She was upset and tried that I should drop this disastrous idea of mine.

I told her that I will try that no one else comes to know about it. But, we needed to warn the girl. "We both can only save her."

She said that she doesn't want to be Shaktiman, and refused to come along.

I went alone to my cousin's home. I waited near the gate for long, reining my anxiousness and preparing for what I will say, how I will say, what I will do if the girl gets upset or cries, and everything else that can happen when I will blast the bomb I was carrying.

"You want to meet someone?" came a voice. I was startled. I looked in the direction of the voice. It was that girl's mother, who probably noticed me standing near the gate. I gathered courage and nodded. "Yes auntie. I have come to meet <girl's name>. I am her friend."

She opened the gate, simultaneously calling the girl. I went in. I said hello little loudly. There was a clear confused look on the face of the girl. But she took me in.

"There is something very urgent I have come to tell you. Please don't get stressed or sad," I immediately whispered. Continuing without a pause I added, "the boy you are friends with, is not serious about you. It is only time pass for him till his classes start."

I stopped with a loud exhalation. I was waiting for an outburst from her, preparing myself to handle it. But what came was a look of surprise and a cool smile.

"It's fine. It's time pass for me too", came a one liner which hit me like a hard punch.

"Do you want to have sharbat?", she asked with a smile. I was too frozen to answer. I just nodded to indicate no.

"Tab theek hai. But, don't tell anyone that I came to tell you this," I managed to mutter and left.

I rushed out and ran home, scolding myself all through for going to her house. I felt like beating myself to make an idiot of me in front of the girl.

My sister was waiting at the gate. She had a worried and an anxious look on her face. Breathing hard, I told her softly what the girl told.

She burst out laughing. The look on her face was shouting clearly, 'I told you so.'

Till today she pulls me for trying to be that unwarranted super hero.

CHAPTER V

#Highway

Have you ever experienced shock, fear, anger, reaction and action – all in a fraction of moment? Anything which makes you wonder what was the actual feeling and emotion at the core of it all!

I was on a road trip with my family. We had just started after a short tea halt enroute. There was a truck in the right lane. We were in the left lane. Little ahead a lady was giving a signal for lift. The truck suddenly swirled left, probably to give her lift. And it barged into the left lane, banging right into the front of our car.

With the screeching sound of brakes, our car stopped. With that came the screaming sound of my children. I looked back terrified, with my heart pounding hard in my ears. My daughter had her lip bleeding. My son had hit on the car door. Both were crying loudly. I looked front. Our car was all dented and bent. And there it was the truck, standing few meters ahead of us.

Totally shaken and panicked, I calmed and settled the children. My husband stepped out and was checking the damage. I saw the truck still standing.

I opened the car door and dashed straight towards the truck. My husband shouted and asked me to stay in. But, I didn't. Seeing me coming, the driver jumped down. I shouted on him asking, "Why are you driving if you don't know how to drive. What if something would have happened to my children. You wait here till police comes." Saying this I climbed on the truck. He sat on the road and said, "theek hai. I will wait. Waise kuch hona nahi hai."

I then noticed the key in the truck. I took it out, jumped down and came to our car.

We stayed there for a long time, at least it seemed so. The truck driver too sat comfortably on the road seeing us struggling with our car.

Continuous guru-gyaan poured from my husband all through our effort to free the stuck bonet and wheel. Finally, the car obliged and started. Moving with an irritating scratching sound, it managed to take us to a mechanic shop couple of kilometers down the road.

And about the truck keys! I tossed it towards the truck driver as we left.

And the swirl of all emotions in that fraction, resonated with how swiftly our journey changed on that highway.

CHAPTER VI

#Bully's Bully

Have you ever been a bully against the bullies? Andar se kaanpte hue, par upar se garajte hue.

This is from the days of the retro era. The days when the screen was only Doordarshan. The days of the dialler phones, which were kept locked to protect from the misuse by neighbours. Also, the days when milk didn't come in a packet to your door steps.

Those days we had to go to a dairy with a 'dole' in hand, place it in the long queue of 'doles' and wait for the turn of our 'dole'. As the doles will patiently move ahead, we will anxiously peep to check if the bucket has enough to last till the turn of our dole. If it doesn't, we will have to sit there waiting as the 'uncle' again fills the bucket by squeezing milk from the buffaloes and till it is the turn of our dole.

As for all the house chores, the days for this daily trip to the dairy were also divided between the siblings.

Once, my elder sister came back home crying with empty dole. She told our mother that some children on the way always call her names from inside their house. That day they made their dog bark at her. She got scared, ran and came back.

Our mother was worried about the milk getting over and dairy closing. She told her to ignore them and quickly go and bring milk.

She was not ready. I was rushed, out of my turn, to get milk.

Next day on my turn, she had to go as per the roster. She refused to go alone. I offered to join. Not for any interest to get milk, but to know who are troubling and scaring my sister.

On the way she showed me the house. It was a corner house in the lane just behind our house. Two girls, similar to our ages, lived there. Their parents normally returned late from work. As was the protocol for children in those days, they also stayed locked inside when parents were out. They will stand at the window during the evening. When my sister passed, they would shout calling her names, making scary sounds and making their dog bark on her.

Waiting for the turn of our 'dole' that day we deliberated on various ways to stop them.

Asking our parents to interfere was not an option as neighbours that time didn't fight over children matters. "If we will tell they will think we are 'cry babies' and laugh on us." I said, adding "We will only handle them. Let's go."

"They have a dog. They will leave it on us. We should now come from a different route," my sister suggested.

"Why will we take a longer route because of them. We will go and talk to them. You hold the dole and stand ahead. If they will leave the dog I will shout. You run away with milk. I will come."

With our plan made, we reached outside their house to execute it.

I stood in front of their gate and my sister went ahead. I knocked on the gate. There was no sound. I knocked again louder. Sound of the dog barking inside came. I was little scared. But I knocked again, calling loudly, "aunty...aunty." Couple of times I called again, every time my pitch going higher than earlier. I could see the curtain of the window moving. Then someone from behind the curtain said, "aunty is not there."

The voice seemed worried. And it gave me the much-needed strength. I said loudly, "Aunty is not there that's why you are teasing and scaring my sister. Come out and scare me. I am coming inside and I will not go till aunty comes. I will tell aunty what you are doing every day."

I banged the door handle harder. Two voices came, "OK. We will not do again. Don't come or tell mummy."

I was actually scared to go inside. Still, I shouted, "Next time you will call my sister anything, I will make your 'bharta' and tell aunty. And tell that to your dog also."

I rushed from there and ran to my sister standing in the lane. We both held our hands tight and ran home as if the dog was chasing us.

Next few days I still went along, though behind her, just to check if our plan worked.

And it did.

CHAPTER VII

#Flame of Faith

Have you ever lived the power of that invisible Almighty, which the self-proclaimed logical beings argue to show and prove. Kuch aisa, jiska reason samajhna aur samjhana possible nahi hai. Some can call it a mere 'co-incidence', but for you it is pure faith.

The day started like any other usual day. After hurriedly sending my children to school, I left for work. I was driving when I got a call about the cancellation of my daughter's evening class. Courtesy query about the teacher's health gave a shocking piece of information. A toddler in my neighbourhood was critical in the hospital. Hearing about what happened numbed me till my core.

I had seen the child happily enjoying just a couple of days back. And now I was hearing this. I reached to my work place struggling to grasp what I had heard. I could not hold myself together at work. I took emergency permission from my senior and started to go to the hospital.

Those days most phones were not smart. As asking way was common, I kept checking for the hospital address every few hundred meters through the narrow traffic laden lanes.

Once at the hospital reception, I collected myself and enquired based on the piece of information I had. I was guided to a floor. I could see the family, some of them pacing up and down behind the doctor and nurses, and some sitting on the bench. The stress and worry clearly written all over their faces.

I could not gather the strength to go and talk to them. I sat quietly on a bench in the waiting area. I kept sitting for couple of hours there and then quietly left.

I came back home and was too overwhelmed to hold myself. I called my mother, my forever go to person in all such overwhelming moments. Crying inconsolably, I told her about the incident. She tried to pacify me but I just was not listening. She was consoling me that all will be fine, and I was continuously questioning her about God and why something like this should happen. Her all efforts and explanations were failing to help. Her Geeta Gyan, and our limitation to perceive God's wish etc did little to calm me down. She told me to pray and rest for some time.

I kept sitting and crying in front of my temple area for long. I don't know suddenly what happened. I was little angry. I got up and lighted a diya. I said, "If you have done this, it is not right. Now you will only have to correct it. This diya will light till the child doesn't come back home. And if you will not bring the child back to the mother, a diya will never light again here."

The child was home in a month.

Was it the power of faith, or merely a co-incidence? Why it should have happened?

I have not found an answer even today, as I had none that day.

CHAPTER VIII

#Mother Promise

We hear, read and imagine miracles all the time. But, have you ever experienced and lived a miracle? Kuch aisa jo IMPOSSIBLE se I M POSSIBLE ho gaya!

For as long as I remember my life, I had an instant connect with children. From my own childhood days, I would joyfully readily babysit my younger siblings, children of my elder siblings and even those of our neighbours too.

After my marriage, I was eager to have my children. But every month the excitement would turn to disappointment. The wait was making me anxious.

We were in a small town for my husband's project. On my insistence, we visited our hometown for a checkup. We visited a hospital and were put through multiple tests and scans. The doctor met us after the reports and threw a bomb by declaring that it was not possible for us to have a child naturally.

I was hearing something I had never thought in my wildest dreams. I sat with great effort. The doctor went on to explain the options of treatment, chances and related costs.

Those were the times with limited and long treatment options, at high costs with low success rates. We kept sitting out for long, calculating the amount of funds we would need to arrange, and weighing it against the probability of success.

My head did agree with my husband that we should not get into all this. But my heart was playing a different beat.

Hoping that it might be wrong, we directly went to our family doctor with the reports. He too confirmed what we had already heard. He said, "you should not worry about this. You have studied and worked so hard. You should focus on your career now."

We had the train back for the same evening. We rushed home and informed our families about the verdict of the doctors. As we were leaving, my in-laws told me not to worry, and assured that they will not blame me for this.

As we were about to leave, my parents came rushing. They told us to take care of each other and gave me a small packet. I hugged them with teary eyes and we left.

As the train started moving, I opened the packet. It had a medicine bottle and a slip with details on using it. I closed the packet and kept it.

I tried to engage myself in whatever activities I could find to do in that remote place. He was busy with his project.

We were obviously not talking about it, but were definitely thinking about it.

After a couple of months my parents came to visit us. Their presence gave us the much-needed support in those times. They both would cook, take us out for walks and engage us in fun conversations.

After a couple of weeks, it was time for them to leave. As their taxi came, my mom took out money and gave to me. I refused to take.

Mom said, "Don't say no. When I go to didi's place I give to children there also. So, take it."

I said, "You give to children. I don't have any, and might not have too. So, why will I take."

Before I could complete, I was crying. My father had tears in his eyes. Tears were flowing from my mother's eyes too. She hugged me tight and said, "Kaise nahi hoga. Matarani hai. Just see. Nine months and you will have your baby in your lap."

With moist eyes, my husband and my father made me and mom sit in the cab. We all were quiet on the way to the station. My parents left and we returned back.

My husband was upset. He said, "It was not right. You should have managed yourself better. They came all the way here to support us and you sent them back crying."

I too was sad and felt guilty. I tried my best to put a strong voice in my next weekly calls with them. I knew they were also doing the same.

But the month after we were shockingly surprised.

And nine months after I heard, "Congratulations. You have got a doll as your birthday gift."

And two years later, our doll got a younger sibling.

You may call it a miracle, manifestation or a mere coincidence. I know it is Only My Ma.

CHAPTER IX

#The Apple Saga

Have you ever felt a simple normal thing turning into a dreaded thorn for your entire life. Koi aisi cheez jo dekhte hi your senses scream and your heart aches?

I was in the second trimester of my first pregnancy. It was a magical blessing amidst a 'not possible' situation with its own share of tears and heartaches. My husband was again out for an official tour and I was at my in-law's place. My morning sickness was still continuing with frequent bouts of vomiting. I had the schedule of my gynaecologist's appointment in the morning. My father-in-law didn't drive. My father had to come to take me for the check-up. I had asked my mother-in-law if she will come along. She had refused.

The next morning, as any other normal day I checked with my mother-in-law about what breakfast shall I make. She told me to check with my sister-in-law and make whatever we both want to eat. I said, "If I will eat now, I will vomit in the car. I will eat after the check-up." She said, "You then get ready. Eat some fruit and go. We will decide what we will eat."

I took bath and did my morning prayer. My mother-in-law was sitting on the bed reading a book.

I took an apple in a plate, came and sat near her. I started cutting it. I ate 2 or 3 slices and started feeling nauseated. I said, "mummyji I am not able to eat. I am feeling like vomiting. You take it please." She said, "People eat so much during this time and you are not able to eat one apple. Finish it."

I took one more bite but could not eat. I said I won't be able to. "Please you eat it. I am not able to," I said.

Just then my sister-in-law entered, screaming at top of her voice, "If you think this is a 'sarai', you don't have to live here. Pack your stuff and leave right now."

I was shell shocked. I looked at my mother-in-law. She was quiet. I said, "what happened? What have I done?"

My sister-in-law screamed, "whole house is waiting for breakfast and this madam is sitting and eating like a queen."

I looked at my Mother-in-law and said, "I had asked and you told you will decide later."

My mother-in-law replied, "Yes. When you went to take bath, we also decided to eat fruits for breakfast. But you started eating without asking. You should have first checked again with us before eating."

I wanted to say how I would have known this, or she could have told me when I came and sat near her. But there was no room for this. My sister-in-law was shouting and screaming at top of her voice, pacing up and down the room. All through hurling the words of abuse I had never heard in my life.

I asked my mother-in-law to ask her to stop. She said, "She is not telling anything wrong. You have not been giving the right kind of importance in-laws should get." On this my sister-in-law now started shouting all sorts of abusive words for my parents. She went on from how I am ill fit in the family to how my parents have raised spoilt children and how they are not teaching me to adjust and what not.

This verbal bombarding with intermittent banging of dishes and doors continued for long. I could hear loud honking in between. After sometime I realised it could be my father who had to come to pick me. I took my medical file and walked out.

I sat hurriedly in the car. My father asked what happened. I just said, "chalo" and started crying loudly.

Instead of the clinic he took me home to my mom.

I was rolling out floods sharing what all I heard. I was more upset after knowing that my father was listening all this standing with my father-in-law outside. But, neither of them came in to intervene.

My father was teary eyed. He said that he did request my father-in-law to go in and stop. But he refused telling, "It is ladies' matter. They will only sort it."

I burst crying, "I am your daughter, not his. You didn't think if something would happen to me or my baby?"

My mother was also very upset. She asked me to send a message to my husband that she wants to talk to him.

I sent him an email. He called in the night. They both spoke.

Overwhelmed with fear and anxiety, riddled with doubt on their assurances, I was dropped back in the night.

Whatever happened that day between morning and evening, and also in the night and days that followed, set the tone of many things for the future. But, two things stuck with me vividly. One, the capacity of an Indian parent of a girl for quietly hearing and bearing standing right outside, what happened that day inside. Two, the snow white's pain at the sight of an apple after it stuck in her throat. Forever.

CHAPTER X

#Five Day Wife

Have you ever experienced something which makes you wonder 'what was it!' 'Why did it happen!'

And you are still searching the answers which you will never get.

***Flash Match-Making**

I was 20 years old in the second year of my graduation. Our family was a middle-class service family. The next door neighbours had their business. Being together for years, they had been like our extended family, as most neighbours used to be in those days.

On one winter month's late afternoon, the neighbours called my mother. She went out and soon came back excited and panting.

She spoke to my father. He spoke to my grandparents. And, I was called.

I was told that the neighbours have proposed for my marriage to one of their immediate relatives.

I shot back yelling that I will not do and that I wanted to study.

But I only heard, "They will allow you to complete your studies." "After you we need time to prepare for the marriage of your younger sister too". "They are a good family. We know them for so many years." "They are coming forward and asking for it. Please say Yes."

I tried to argue and convince. But together they took "as you think right", from me.

Within couple of hours everything was set. Before the date could change in the calendar, I was engaged after the customary 'seeing' and 'meeting' of ten minutes.

I had seen this all around me. I knew it was normal for an average middle class girl. But what would follow, I neither knew nor imagined.

Next few days I went to college anxious. I was worried about anyone coming to know about my engagement. I dreaded anyone knowing that I will be the first one to get married, when always I said about studying more and doing more.

I avoided talking to anyone. I had always been the one entering the class before time and sitting on the first bench. Now I would enter the class late, take the last seat and leave before anyone would get up to leave.

But friends being friends, they soon took it out of me.

They heard it and sided with me. And then showed their excitement on this big news. We celebrated in the college canteen with campa and bhelpuri.

Ten months till the D Day flew fast in trying to complete as much portion of the syllabus, as many notes and as many college files possible.

In college circle the discussion was around what colour should I wear, how many days leave I should take, where should I go after marriage and what should I gift him on which days.

In family the buzz was around what to buy, what to arrange and whom all to invite.

Various rituals and functions, and I was married. Everyone was happy.

#Day 1: As a young bride, I too was excited. Before that I had never worn makeup and not dressed up like this. I was liking myself in a beautiful bright saree, wearing lipstick and bindi. I was stealing a glance of myself every time I passed any mirror in that house.

The day went attending to all the rituals lined up in my new house. In the night was the reception.

For hours we were standing on stage, greeting the guests and posing for a picture with each group. He seemed irritated. He was repeatedly calling my neighbour aunty, who was our match-maker. He would make a strange face and pass comments to her about the people at the reception. I didn't like it and was trying to pretend that I didn't hear.

I was very hungry and tired and wanted to now sit and eat. When it finally seemed to be done, and I was hoping to be taken for food, he turned and rushed to the back on the stage. I panicked, went near him and asked what happened.

"A mosquito went in my mouth," he said, trying to do vomit. The match-maker aunty and few others joined. Someone was rubbing his back, someone was asking him to drink some water and some others were standing with me seeing him angrily refusing to swallow anything till he vomits the mosquito out.

He insisted on going home. Aunty asked if I would go along or want to eat. I told I am very hungry and want to eat something. He said, "Quickly make her eat and send us home fast."

We were taken to the dining area. Our plate was set. He told me to eat fast. I had always been a slow eater. But I was trying to grab quick bites and swallowing fast, forgetting the mannerism expected of a bride at her reception. Despite this he was continuously telling aunty, "Tell her to finish fast". She was seeing my effort and was trying hard to keep him quiet and calm. After taking some bites and spoons, as I felt little better, I said I am done.

He got up and we immediately came home with aunty.

We were taken to a room on the terrace. Aunty said our room was occupied by guests so we would have to stay in that room for the night. The room was stuffed with big boxes, suitcases, piles of bedsheets, blankets and extra marriage stock. It had a bed in the middle with rose petals spread on it.

Aunty came with a big glass of milk. She told him to drink it and went. He started drinking it. Surprised, I said, "but that mosquito?" He said, "It's not coming out. I will see it in the morning," extending the glass to me he continued, "half is for you. You drink." I made a face and said, "I don't like milk. This also has so much cream. And, I can't drink from the same glass. I will vomit." He gave a glance and drank the whole milk.

I went to change. When I came back, he was snoring loudly. I too was tired but could not go to bed amidst all the clutter around. Very quietly I shifted and sorted all the stuff scattered around. Once the room was somewhat set, I removed the petals from my side of the bed and lied down. Within seconds I was fast asleep.

#Day 2: Suddenly I felt some touch down. I woke up with a jerk. He was sitting at the edge of the bed and raising my gown up. In a sudden reflex, I kicked him.

He fell down the bed. I said loudly, "what are you trying to do?"

He got up and signalled me to be quiet. He said, "Talk softly. It's morning. Everyone will listen outside."

I was angry. I said, "I will call everyone and tell what you were doing." He said, "they will not tell me anything, but will laugh at you only."

Just then there was a knock at the door. He opened. His cousin was there. She said we need to get ready and come down. He went down with her. I too quickly got ready and came down.

My elder sister had come to take me for the customary 'pug-phera'. I desperately wanted to go home. The ten minutes distance to my home seemed a long stretch that day. As I entered, all the relatives and guests started hugging me and asking if I was happy. I smiled and nodded.

I was eagerly moving behind my mother as she was busy seeing off the guests. As soon as I saw her alone in the kitchen, I went and stood near her. She asked if everything is fine. I nodded. She said, "did something happen in the night?" I was just waiting for her to ask this. I told the complete story from the mosquito trauma to my kicking him, in one breath.

"You hit him! Are you mad!" she blurted. She called my elder sister. She said, "You didn't tell her anything! She hit him and came." My sister gave me a long look. I was confused on what I did wrong. I said, "he was trying to do the wrong thing. I didn't hit him. I just kicked him away."

Looking at my sister, my mother said, "take her inside and talk to her. Explain her something."

My sister took me in our room and closed the room. She asked me to tell what happened and what I did. I told her also everything. She scolded me for kicking and asked if I didn't learn anything in the science class or from any of my friend.

By now I was irritated. I shouted, "what my class has to do with what he did? How any friend will know or tell. No one's family was in such a hurry like you all."

She went to my mother and said, "She doesn't know anything. I don't know where to start and how to explain your daughter. I can't do it." "You are elder to her. You only can do it. Go beta. Please tell her,"my mother said.

I was angry on what was going on between them. I told them to stop this cryptic talk and tell clearly what is the matter.

My sister told me to go and sit in the room and allow them to think. Angry, I went and slept off.

My sister came and woke me up. My brother-in-law was with her. She closed the door. She said that they want to talk to me. I nodded and sat at the edge of the bed. They sat on chairs across me.

He began, "It is very odd for me to talk to you on something I am going to talk now. But I will take it as a doctor explaining something to you." I looked at my sister, and him. I was now stressed with the gravity of the tension on their faces. I nodded quietly and sat straight.

He began by taking few body parts names and asked if I know them. Then he asked as a science student, if I have studied the reproductive system. I nodded yes. He said, "this will make it easy for me to explain." Using the scientific nomenclature and terms, he then outlined the need of intercourse for this process to be complete and successful.

I nodded. He left.

My sister and mother asked if it's clear to me now. I said, "but, what about my studies?" They were visibly irritated with me now. My sister said, "that will also happen. It is not going to stop with this." My mother said, "now go and say sorry to him for what you did yesterday."

Filled with guilt, I nodded yes.

When I came back, I was shown my room. It had the bed, dressing and cupboard given by my parents in marriage. My suitcases and his clothes were also kept near the bed. I set the cupboard and dressing. I stacked the suitcases and cleaned the room.

I was waiting for him to come. I wanted to tell sorry. He came late and came straight to the room. He sat on the bed near me. I started crying. He got up and said, "I didn't do anything now!"

I said, "I am sorry for kicking you yesterday."

He smiled and said, "So today you will not kick me".

Crying, I nodded 'No'.

We ate dinner with all and came back to our room. I was sitting on bed. He was pacing up and down the room. I asked what happened. He came on bed, held my hands tight and said, "You will take care of me. Tell me you will not let anything happen to me. You will make me fine."

I was shocked. I was scared. He was repeating these as he was pressing me hard. His grip was now hurting me.

I felt I cannot take any more mystery after spending the whole day in solving why my kick the previous night was wrong. I tried to hold myself upright and asked him what happened.

He said, "I can't tell anything. Everyone has strictly told not to share with anyone. They said it will all get fine after marriage. You promise me you will make me fine."

"I can't help unless I know what is it. If you will tell then we can do something," I replied.

He then started sharing the health issues he was facing. Also, that it is very painful for him to sit. The entire day he keeps standing to avoid this pain. He took some treatment but it was stopped fearing everyone will come to know and it will be harder for him to get married.

I asked when and how he came to know about all these conditions. He shared about the multiple test reports. I told him to show the reports. He said he can't as the file is kept on top of the cupboard in his brother's room.

While talking he also shared that his brother kept the room door open in the night. I insisted for him to go and get the report. He was scared. His brother's room was next to our room. I offered to go and bring. He refused to allow me and said that he would try to get it. I stood at our room door, keeping a watch outside. He sneaked into his brother's room and was out in few moments. He entered our room with a big file in his hand. I took the file and started to check. He told me not to tell anyone about this and slept off.

I was checking each page, each scan and each report. I was relying on the summary to make sense of the situation. I could get that there were many things, but could not get the gravity and how to address them.

I kept thinking on how to take this up. I didn't want my parents to get worried, so decided against sharing with them. Since my brother-in-law was in pharma field and regularly met doctors, I thought he can guide and help. Assured of this being the best way, I kept awake whole night waiting for the sun to rise.

#Day 3: I could not wait for long. Early morning I shook him and woke him up. He turned side and kept sleeping. After few minutes I shook him harder and told him to wake up. He opened his eyes and asked what happened. I told him we will go to my sister's house. He angrily got down the bed and refused. "I told you we will not tell this to anyone. I am not coming anywhere," he said in anger. I told him, "You and I don't know which doctor to go to. He can help us. He can show the reports to a doctor and we can get the required treatment started."

He said, "Bhaiya and Bhabhi will be sitting outside. They will not allow us to go. How will we take this file and step out."

Those were winter months. He was wearing a sweater and a jacket. I suggested to keep the file inside his jacket and we can go. He refused. He said, "They will surely stop us. I can't handle it. I won't do it."

We kept sitting in room for some time. He repeating that he will be scolded for all this. I thinking how to take the file.

I got up and told him, "You go, start the scooter and give me a horn. As soon as I come and sit, immediately start. Don't stop even if someone calls."

He went out. I took the file, pressed it under my armpit and wrapped a shawl. I stood ready at the door, waiting for the horn. He honked a loud, long horn. I swiftly dashed out and towards the scooter, crossing his Bhabhi sitting out on the chair. As I sat behind him, she called loudly, "where are you both going so early?"

He started the scooter with a jerk. Waving his hand in air he said loudly, "Mandir."

Riding fast on mostly empty lanes, we reached my sister's house on that cold chilly morning.

Everyone at my sister's place was shocked to see us there so early in the morning. The newly-weds would go to relatives' house on invitation. But here we were – uninvited and surely not dressed as newly-weds.

We greeted everyone. My Didi-Jeejaji immediately took us to their room. As we sat, they asked if all was well.

I briefed them about the situation and gave them the file. I told, "He is in pain. Show this file to the doctor and get his treatment started. Please don't tell this to anyone else."

My Jeejaji asked him few questions related to the file and the symptoms. His reply was brief and not very clear.

Jeejaji assured us that he will take it today only and will then let us know when we will come to my mother's place.

We started back. As soon as we reached home, everyone was waiting in the verandah. Bhabhi asked sternly where did we go. Without looking, and rushing fast he said, "Mandir". She blocked my way and said angrily, "you were not in the mandir. We went there to check."

I saw him going in room and closing the door. Everyone was looking at me. I was quiet. She came near me and sternly asked again.

I firmly said, "I have seen the file."

She had a panic look. Without waiting, I walked straight to the room.

There was silence and evident tension all around. He got ready and went out. I went to take bath and realised my periods had started. I called his cousin and asked for pads. When I came, they gave breakfast to us in single plate.

In my neighbours' house I had seen the girls not doing any work and sitting separate during their period days. I asked to give breakfast to me separate. Everyone sweetly refused and asked us to eat together. I looked at his cousin. She said, "Kha lo. Ek saath khaoge toh pyaar badega." I quietly ate with him.

I asked him to try to come early from work to be able to go and check the update from Jeejaji. He said he won't and left.

After he left his Bhabhi came to talk. She said I should not have given the file to anyone 'ghar ke bahar'. When I said they are not outsiders and that they can guide to a proper doctor. She got little upset and said, "do you think we can't show to the doctor. We have shown to good doctors. There is nothing much he has. It's all in his mind."

I asked, "if this is it why he is having pain and bleeding since so many days. And why all this was not shared with my parents?"

She said, "We will go to whichever doctor you will tell. Don't tell to your parents as they will get unnecessarily stressed."

I stayed quiet.

My neighbour aunties, his cousins and everyone in the house took turns coming to me and sharing various things about everyone in the house. They were doing their best to engage me but my mind was constantly thinking if didi and jeejaji would have been able to meet any doctor and what doctor would have said.

As my neighbour aunties were leaving in the evening, I asked if I can come along with them. They refused that I can only go with him.

He came late from work. I waited for him to have dinner. As he finished, I asked if we can go to check about the reports.

"I am perfectly fine. I have nothing," sitting near me he said and added, "I will show you tonight."

I said, "my periods have started."

As I completed this sentence, he sprang up and dashed out. In a moment he returned with couple of bedsheets. I was still sitting on the bed. He threw the bedsheets on the floor and said, "take this and sit down. You can't be on bed. You will have to sleep down."

I was taken aback with his tone and what he said. I stood up from the edge of the bed, went and sat up near the pillow. Looking at him, I said, "I am not going anywhere. I will not sleep down."

He panicked and said that I have made the whole bed dirty and where will he sleep now. All ladies of the house sleep down during this time. Saying all this he again dashed out of the room.

I clutched the pillow tight in my hands and sat firmly.

In few moments he came back with his Bhabhi. She asked me when did it start. When I said "morning", he shouted, "I ate with her in the morning. What will happen to me now."

Bhabhi said, "Stay quiet. We will take you to temple tomorrow." She turned to me and asked politely, "why you didn't tell in the morning?" I said I told his cousin.

He went and brought his cousin to the room. They asked if she knew. She replied, "She told me but since she wore a light colour saree, I thought it would not have happened. So, I didn't think to tell."

She was scared and he was furious. Bhabhi said, "It's OK. We will tell everyone that it happened in the night. I will manage cleaning everything."

He shouted, "Look at her. She is still sitting on the bed. She is refusing to sleep down. Where will I sleep?"

Bhabhi looked at me. I said, "I can't sleep on the floor. If I have made the bed dirty, he can sleep on the floor. This bed, bedsheet and blanket is given by my parents. I will sleep on this bed only."

She looked at me and was quiet for a moment. She then looked at him anxiously pacing up and down. She said, "it's OK. You sleep in that corner of the bed. Let her sleep in this corner. No one is coming in the room to check where she slept."

He tried to argue but the lingering file effect worked in my favour.

Grudgingly, he slept at the edge of the bed, half hanging down.

I was trying to make sense of everything that had been happening. I was dying to go to my mother. Holding myself tight in the corner of the bed, I don't know when I slept off.

#Day4: I woke up with some sounds. He was getting ready. I said I want to go to meet mummy. He said, "I don't know. Ask bhabi." And without looking he went out.

I quickly took a shower, changed and came out. Bhabhi was in the kitchen. I went near the kitchen. She asked me not to step inside.

I said that I want to go to meet mummy. She said, "For three days you cannot go out. Till tomorrow you stay in the room only. I will give everything there."

Two more days seemed infinite to me. I had to talk to my mother and tell her all I was going through. I gave up the restraint I was holding on to and started crying loudly. I sat down outside the kitchen, pleading to let me go. Maintaining little distance, she asked me not to cry. She said this is the custom for three days of the periods. After that I can go.

I could not stop. I ran back to the room and kept crying. She kept a plate of breakfast near the door and told me to stop crying and eat it. I didn't touch it.

In some time, the neighbour aunty came. Standing at the door of the room she too said that I can't go because of the custom. I kept crying and refused to eat.

In sometime my sister came. Seeing her I started crying loudly. She hugged me and made me eat food. She said that mom has spoken to aunty that they should have informed these customs before and it is difficult for you to take them as we have never seen these in our home. Aunty has assured that it will all be fine. She will explain him too. Since it is the first time, she has asked you to adjust for two days.

While leaving she softly said, "we are also meeting the doctors. We will tell you once you come after two days."

I sat blank for quite some time. I spent the rest of the half day and night lost in everything happening since the D day.

#Day 5: I had been given a separate set of dishes. For these two days, food was 'poured' in them for me. I had to clean them with sand and leave in sun after every use.

I was following all this for two days, and waiting for the day to turn to night, and night to the morning when I will be able to go and meet my mother.

Day 6: I woke up early, took bath and was ready anxiously waiting to go. But, there were some rituals lined up for me. I quietly attended to them all. By afternoon, finally I was dropped to my mother's place.

Seeing mom I started crying. She asked to tell what happened. My father, grandparents, sister all were there. I told everything.

They told they have shown the reports to the doctors. They wanted to meet and get some more tests done. Didi and Jeejaji met him to come with them to the doctor. But he has refused.

They then said, "till we will not get this sorted, we will not send you."

I had not expected to hear this. But these words gave me the relief of finding a stick in the turbulent ocean I was drowning deep into.

I hugged my mother tightly and cried to my heartful. Everyone had tears in their eyes but were holding me firmly.

My mother said, "there is going to be lot of pressure on you for next some days and may be for long time to follow. If you promise not to get weak, then only we will be able to help you."

Though I didn't know what all will follow, but I knew what is now is not right. They again got my yes. But this time from my heart holding a ray of hope.

He came in the night to take me. After dinner, my parents spoke to him about the medical issues and conveyed their decision to send me only after taking doctor's opinion. He went, and in some time came back with our neighbour aunties. My parents told the same thing to them.

They asked them to talk to me alone. My parents looked at me. I agreed.

They came in the room with me and said that my parents are not doing this right. They asked me to come only for one night with them and promised that they themselves will bring me next day morning to go to any doctor for all check-ups. I said that I will only come if my parents will say so. My parents refused. With folded hands they said, "give us few days to check all these things. Then you can surely take her. Till then we will not send her for a minute too."

They went. But came back again with other relatives. Everyone was insisting to send me only for that night. This continued well past midnight. And my parents firmly held their stand.

As my father, uncles and jeejaji were busy taking doctors' opinions; my mother, sisters and grandparents were holding the fort with continuous flow of people coming to convince them to send me.

In the evening my parents called them and also the seniors of the community. They briefed them about the situation and also the doctor's inputs.

The seniors now wanted to talk to me separately. They asked questions about the when and how I came to know about all this, what did I do, if any relation happened between us in these days and some more direct questions. I answered to them all.

They got up and kept their hand on my head. One of them said, "What you are doing has not happened here before. You will face many issues with this. But, never get scared. God Himself has come and helped you all these days there. He will only take care of you now. You are like 'Jhansi ki Rani'. Keep holding your fort!

And the five-day long marriage saga ended.

The days and months ahead did bring issues. It seemed every eye is watching me. It felt everyone is guarding their sons and daughters from me. There were many moments drowning me in turmoil of thoughts, and some driving me nuts. But I sure was a tough nut.

And the fact that my family had my back sailed me through and helped me soar high.

And, they still are our next-door neighbours.

CHAPTER XI

#Settle. Unsettle. Repeat.

My marriage festivities had begun. I was happy as it seemed the new chapter of my life is starting at a high note. He had a good job and also a big house given by the company. I had got my first job and got my base location in the same city.

I had been there around two months before our marriage for my job training. I had seen the house and planned how I will set it. We had met all his friends and even done some of our shopping together.

Ten days before our marriage he called and said that he is planning to take up a new course. If he clears the entrance, he would have to resign from his job. Everyone in my and his family were worried.

Our fathers were sitting and praying that he should not clear the entrance. He failed the first attempt. Our families celebrated.

A week before the marriage he called to tell that he has resigned. He had cleared the entrance. He had to report for his joining three days before the marriage. He vacated the house and went straight for the course. He joined classes for two days and got 'special marriage leaves' for three days.

All the guests were at our homes. At both the houses all the festivities were going on, sans the groom. The cousins were teasing on the unique marriage where groom has a 'guest appearance.' The uncles and aunts were raising eyebrows and asking if 'ALL is WELL'.

Finally, he arrived, a day before the marriage. He came straight to meet me. Mehndi was being put on my hands. He said he wants to talk. I went in the room with him.

Excited, I showed him my mehndi hands. Without looking at them, he said, "Look. I have come to tell to postpone the marriage."

Shocked, I stared at him, and then at the mehndi on my hands. Showing him my hands I said, "Mehndi has been put. Today is our Shagun. All preparations are done. All guests are here. How can I tell my parents that you want to cancel the marriage?"

He said, "I am just telling to postpone it. I have no job right now. All my savings have gone for the fees of the course. I have zero money with me now. I will manage at my friend's place. But I can't keep you there. And I am not sure how long it will take to get the job after the course!"

All my excitement had changed to anxiety. But I surely had no courage to tell this to my parents. I said, "It is hard to go and tell this to my parents now. You do your course. I am sure I will get some job there. Else, I am sure your parents or my parents should be able to keep me here for some more months."

"I will not ask any of them. Also, I don't want to start it this way," he said.

"Then you should have thought, or atleast spoken before doing all this," I replied dryly.

He was quiet. He then said, "OK. Let's do it and see how things go."

I came out to address the stress clearly written on my parent's face. I briefed them about his state, and that he has managed to get only three days off. "He would leave the next day after marriage", I told them.

They all rushed for our Shagun ceremony. This is the ceremony before marriage where the bride's family visits the groom's place with shogun or gifts for the members of the groom's family.

The bride doesn't accompany them for this ceremony. I got the much-needed space and time to be with my thoughts on the new twist of things coming my way.

I was moving around the rooms casually. This was my home for the twenty-three young years of my life. I looked at the attic where I would climb and sit. I smiled at the thought that sitting up we would talk loudly about the comics we would get on rent during our summer holidays. It was our effort to entice the children of our tenants with our story books so that they would be ready to exchange their story books with us. And we always succeeded. I touched the crack in the chair with which I fell when my younger sibling pulled and left it. I looked at everything I had set in the garage, turned into my room. I was sad that my sibling will now have all this, and I will no longer be able to fight over them.

But where will I live, how long, what will I do was all unclear to me.

He had told that it was highly unlikely that he would get a job in the same city, as his course had no opportunities there. I knew I can't ask for relocation again, that too when there is no clarity on the time and place I would be going to. Thinking about all this, I slept off even before everyone came back from my Shagun.

I woke up early in the morning. There were some rituals lined up for the marriage. In the afternoon my parents informed me that they have booked his flight ticket. Instead of going by train the day after marriage, he would now be able to stay one day extra.

• • •

Our marriage was in the temple. It was a simple ceremony with our family members and close friends. He didn't want the usual band, baja, barat. He came in a car. After marriage was the reception in a beautiful garden in our city. We were happy, enjoying the moments together with our friends and family.

We came back to his house at dawn. After resting for few hours, we got busy in the rituals, meeting the guests and seeing them off. We went to visit our grand-parents as he was leaving the next morning. Everyone told him to come and take me quickly.

There were no flights from our city then. We all went to drop him at the bus stop. He had five hours bus journey to reach the airport. As the bus came, he gave me a tight hug and left.

Next couple of days I engaged myself in seeing his old photographs and listening about them from my in-laws.

I sent message to my manager about the inability to join due to my new uncertain situation.

In some days he informed that he has taken a small room near his friend's place. But it had no provision of a kitchen or a separate bathroom. Also, the owner had given the room for single person only.

My father had been insisting that I should go to him. I was hesitant. My father said, "ek se do hote hain toh sab raste nikal jaate hain. Kuch din dekho, nahi jugaad baithe toh waapis aa jaana."

I spoke to him about it. He agreed and told me to plan only for a week. "I have no money. The owner will not allow two people for more than a week. I am full day busy in the institute. Still if you want, come. But for only a week."

My father spoke to my in-laws to take me to him. They refused and asked him to drop me. My father booked the tickets. My mother gave me five thousand rupees to take along to manage things there. I refused saying that he will not like it if I will take it from them.

The night before we had our train, my parents came to my in-law's place. They gave an envelope with five thousand rupees. They told them, "This is the money her friends and relatives gave for her on the wedding. We will not keep it. Children will need it in a new place. So, we brought to give it to her."

My mother-in-law said, "It is for your daughter. You give her. She can take with her there."

My parents were happy that they have given me something to manage in a new place, and they gave it officially.

As I entered in the room after seeing off my parents at the gate, I saw my sister-in-law pacing up and down the room. She was angry and asking my father-in-law to give money to clear the pending bill of wedding photography. My father-in-law refused that he has no more money to give. My mother-in-law was angry over how he can refuse to take the responsibility of clearing the wedding expenses. He was arguing that why the videographer was booked if there was no budget for it. All the arguments, counter-arguments and shouting continued for some time, their pitch and tone turning louder and harsher with every minute.

I was very stressed hearing all this. I had not seen anything of this kind any time before. Scared and hesitant, I intervened and slowly asked, "we can use this five thousand if it will be enough."

"Bill is five thousand only. But this money has come as your wedding gift. We can't take it," my mother-in-law said.

"It's OK. Clearing the bill is more urgent," I said and gave the envelope to her.

She took it and immediately everything became calm.

Empty hand but heart brimming with excitement, I started with my father the next morning.

• • •

All through the thirty hours long journey he told me the stories of his hardship days during the early job years. He shared his odd schedule of travel and how my mother's support helped him and the family. Last few hours of the journey went in him explaining me to find a job and manage to stay together.

"I have brought you. Now you have to find a way to stay here. That will only help you both have a strong bond," he said, adding, "call if you need any help, but try to manage and support him here."

We reached late in the evening. He came to pick us. We went to his friend's house and had dinner. Dad stayed there for the night and we went to the room he had taken.

It was a small room at the back of an independent house. It had an inbuilt shelf in one wall and a double bed in the middle. Its access was through a narrow corridor on one side of the house. There was a narrow empty space at the back of the room. The toilet and bathroom were on the other side of the house. One had to cross the corridor, and the front of the house, and the similar corridor on the other side of the house to use it. All these didn't matter a bit. We both were happy to be finally together.

Early morning his friend came to our room with my father. They brought a gas cylinder along.

Dad had seen spare gas cylinders at his house. He spoke to his father and requested to lend one for some time. Obviously, he readily agreed. And, here it came.

He asked, "But, what will we do with this? There is no kitchen and stove here."

"Chai toh ghar par piyenge," my father said, adding, "when you will come back from your class, we will have tea together here."

He seemed confused. He said, "don't set much. I have told owner for a week only."

He and his friend left for their classes.

As soon as they left my father asked me to get ready to go out. We went exploring the neighbourhood. He took me to a store and bought some vegetables, eggs, milk, grocery, bucket, baskets and mop. He showed me around a medical store, a STD booth, vegetable shop and also an auto stand. I was quietly listening to him explaining about the lanes and stops that seemed safe as per him and where we should not go late. We stopped at a small hotel on the way and ate lunch.

We came back to the room, carrying bags loaded with around a week's stuff. Dad then opened the bag he had carried along from home. Out from it came a burner, all the basic utensils and also the basic dry cereals, spices, flour etc enough for around a month.

I was surprised at how my parents had prepared to help me settle in my 1st house away from our home. So what if it was only a small room. Before I could think more, dad called out to me to start setting my first 'kitchen'.

Soon we had old newspapers spread on the floor in one corner of the room. On one we had put a basket with packets of dry ingredients and a basket with vegetables. On other we had set the utensils. Near the gas stove was a small stool to sit and cook.

Once the set-up was done, dad went and brought the bucket filled from the bathroom on the other side of the house and kept it in the little space at the back of the room. We then got down to inaugurate our kitchen. We first boiled the milk. Next was a cooker whistling away happily with the Toor dal simmering in it. The wok had aloo-gobhi getting ready. As I was making dough ready, dad cut the salad.

After we had kept the dinner ready, I asked dad to rest. Tired after the long journey and a busy day, he dozed off. I went to take bath and got ready. Dad was awake by then. We were waiting for him to come.

He was more shocked than we were expecting seeing our kitchen in the room. He was worried about how the owner will take this. He said, "She is here for only a week. Why you have spread all this for a week?"

Dad said, "One week you both will have to eat. So, make and eat at home. Uske baad ki baad mein dekhenge. Now, don't worry so much. Let's enjoy dinner."

I made hot rotis. Dad roasted papads. We all enjoyed a hearty meal, all through sharing our exploration of the place during the day. After dinner we went to drop dad to his friend's place to sleep. He shared with them about our adventurous act of setting up a kitchen in the room. They all had good fun with dad. His friend said that morning tea he will have in our kitchen before going to the class.

As he was busy getting ready to go, his friend and dad came. I had prepared upma. We all took breakfast with a hot cup of tea. They both rushed for their class. Dad went to explore the city. My day went in cleaning utensils, setting room, and scrubbing the little back space which will be my washing area. All through I was trying to work without much noise and with minimum water possible, fearing the landlord getting upset. I ate some upma left from breakfast for lunch.

Dad was back by evening. He told few things about the city as we had tea. We prepared dinner together.

His friend joined us for the dinner. We were discussing about this new unique experience of cooking in a small corner of the room, and sitting and eating there too. We had to wind up fast as dad was leaving early morning the next day.

We went to drop dad in the morning. He said, "she might come behind you in a week."

Dad said, "abhi toh enjoy karo. Meri beti hai. Ek week mein rehene ka koi jugad kar legi!"

• • •

After seeing off dad, he went for his class. I went around checking for any office spaces or places to work. I could not find anything around, except the shops and stores.

When he returned in the night, he had a newspaper with job openings. He had taken it from the library of his institute. He had two openings circled in it. One was nearer to the place we were staying and the other was far. We decided that I should first try for the one nearer.

Before leaving for the class, he explained me the address and its approximate location. I got ready, took my certificates file and left. I took an auto and reached at the location. I was nervous.

The building seemed old. I checked about the address from the shop near the building. I went inside. The stairs were narrow. The office was on the third floor. Hesitantly, I showed the newspaper cutting of the opening to the person sitting outside on the stool. He pointed at a desk and asked me to sit.

It was an empty small room with some tables and chairs kept all around the walls. For long I sat there waiting. He then asked me to go inside. It was again a small room adjacent to the room I was waiting in. It had a big table in the middle. On the other side of it was a young man sitting on a chair. I wished him. He pointed at a chair and signalled for me to sit. As I sat, he kept his legs on the table. Trying to stay confident, I gave my file to him. He didn't take note of it. He lighted a cigarette and started smoking. "You have got this job. You can come from tomorrow," he said staring at me.

I was very uncomfortable. I said, "thank you sir. But, please check my certificates to be sure if I fit the work."

"I don't need certificates to know who can do the work. I am sure you will do it well. You will get Rs 6000/," he said, leaning back on the chair same way and smoking.

I took my file. Standing up I said, "Thank you sir. I will surely consider."

"I can give more also if you come from tomorrow," he said.

I will talk to my husband once and accordingly confirm." I said and left.

I rushed fast the other room, almost running down the stairs. I hurried for an auto and reached home. It took me some time to get my heart beat and breath back in order.

"Rs 6000/ is good enough money for us to stay put and manage. He might be from a rich family, so could have been casual. Just think once are you over analysing him," my husband said when I told him about the 'interview'.

"I am not getting the right feeling. I will try at the other place tomorrow," I said.

Next day was his off. We went to try for the other opening circled in the newspaper. It took us around thirty minutes to reach in an auto. It was a big auto showroom in the busy business area. I went in. There were some more people sitting for the interview. Soon it was my turn.

It was a big and clean office. An elderly person was sitting on the other side of the big table. I wished him. He smiled, wished and asked me to sit. I gave him my file. He took it and checked my certificates. "You have impressive credentials and seem to be hardworking with what all you have done. You seem to be just married," pointing at my wedding bangles he said. "This job has long hours. Why you want to apply for this job?" he asked.

I was in desperate need of a job. And I didn't have the guts to tell of my situation, as that will indicate the uncertainty around the duration of my stay in that city.

"My husband has long working hours. I feel very bored sitting alone. I want to work and stay busy," I said.

"We will be happy to have you here. We will be able to offer Rs 3000/. You can join from Monday," he said.

"Thanks a lot for the offer. But this is too less. Most of it will go in auto only," I replied, disheartened.

"You said you want to work just to keep yourself busy. Still, I will make it Rs 3200/. We will also give you our new launch gear bike to commute. We will take care of the petrol too. So, the complete amount will be your pocket money to enjoy," he said.

"Thank you. I think I will take it. But, is it fine if I talk to my husband once and confirm?" I asked fearing losing the offer.

He smiled and said, "sure. You can come at 9:00 AM on Monday if you want to join."

Happy and smiling, I thanked him and left.

He was waiting out. I told him about the interview and the offer in the auto on the way back home.

He said, "think one more time. This is half of the amount compared to the amount you were offered yesterday. It will be very hard for us to manage in this amount. Also, this place is far and work hours are more. It will be difficult to ride the gear bike in traffic. Soon the monsoon months will start, and rains here are heavier. You can join there and try for some days."

"I don't have the right gut feel about that guy and place. I won't be comfortable to go and work there. Other things I will manage. It is for around three months only. Shall we try to manage in less, choked with emotions I asked holding his hands.

He gave me a tight hug and nodded.

That night we went to a STD booth. In a quick call, with eyes glued to the running meter, I informed my mother about the offer. She was happy. "Don't hesitate to call if you need anything any time. We are always there. Take care of both of you," she said. "I will. But, how to wash shirts and pants with hands?" I worriedly asked. "Soak for some time and brush the collar and cuffs little," she replied. I hurriedly said OK and kept the phone.

• • •

I was little stressed next day thinking about my wardrobe. I had brought just 5 dresses and 2 sarees. Just one month into my marriage, they were definitely not simple work dresses. I knew I had no choice, but to manage with these. I fixed each dress for a day of the week. Saree was kept as flexible option for anything special.

Monday morning my husband dropped me while going to his institute.

The showroom had just opened. There was a person cleaning the place. I sat on the sofa in the waiting area, checking the pamphlets and brochures kept there. Soon the staff started coming in. A tall and slender person came to me and introduced himself as the manager. I wished him and introduced myself. He asked me to join him to meet the MD. We went to his office.

After doing the customary documentation he took me around the showroom, explaining about the various departments, process and my work. He introduced me to the staff and showed my desk. He gave some papers and files and asked me to spend the day reading through them. The papers had the details about the company and specifications about different bikes at the showroom.

I opened the file and started reading through it. It all was very new for me. For some hours I tried to read and memorize the specifications and details given to me. Then I got tired and felt that I was dozing off. I got up, moved around and went to the person on the display floor. I requested him to explain the specifications with the model. He readily agreed and enthusiastically explained the details. This was the routine for the next few days. To avoid mixing up the specifications, I would practice by writing them in my notebook.

I would reach every day before my time. In the evening, my eyes would be oscillating between my desk and the clock on the wall. The moment it's hands would stretch themselves straight and tall, my hands would grab my bag and I would dash out. Within seconds I would be on the bike given to me, rushing on the road to home.

Reaching home, I would immediately cook food, clean the room, wash clothes, take bath and wait for him. As soon as he would come, we would have dinner. I would be so hungry that I would not even allow him to change. After dinner we would sit in the small space behind the room to wash dishes. As I would be washing dishes, he would sing songs while pouring water on the dishes to help me clean them.

We would spend lot of time sitting at the edge of that wall, scrubbing and cleaning those six-seven dishes. The dishes which we would have mostly cleaned already by finger licking every bit of food on it. These moments seemed to wash away the day's tiredness more than those dishes.

Some songs seemed to touch me more than others. Every time he would ask me which songs, I would never be able to recall the lyrics. I would just say, "woh mere waala. The ones you were singing while washing dishes." And he would always remember that and sing them again for me. He would sing them on our strolls in the lanes near our house, and also sitting on the edge of the lake we would go every Sunday evening. With a cone of roasted chana we would sit there for hours, talking about his course and my week at work. He enjoyed talking, and singing. And, I listening to him.

• • •

In hard times things never go as you want them to go. Around two weeks into the job, and the house owner called my husband. He came back and said, "he wants us to vacate the house in two weeks." The house owner only wanted a single person in the room and was not happy with us both staying.

We started our search for another house. His friend lived in that area and we had to find something nearby. Since they sat together till late every night to study and complete their assignments, staying far was not an option. Every night after dinner we would scan couple of lanes around the area to find a 'for rent' board. We would check with every shop keeper too, hoping to get some input on the available rooms or houses. We did find some but the rent was beyond our means.

One night on our routine search patrol, we saw a two storeyed building. The ground floor front room was visible from the road as the curtains were not drawn. There was an elderly couple watching television in the room. I told him, "this building is big and seems to have many rooms. Let us go and check with them, if they can give us any room."

We knocked at the main gate. After knocking couple of times, we noticed the uncle peeping from the window. I said loudly, "Namaste uncle. Can I please talk for two minutes." uncle opened the door and came out. Behind him aunty also came. We wished them. I said, "We are new to the city. He is studying and I have a small job. We are looking for a small room to stay. Do you have any available in the building, or you know some place where we can get one? It will be of great help."

"We live on ground floor. Our children are out. But, first floor has their things. They stay there whenever they visit. Second floor is also vacant. But it is not cleaned as we don't use it. You can check it if you are fine to take it."

"We will not need the complete floor. Only one room will be enough for us," I said fearing high rent again.

"Separate room we don't have. Only second floor we can give," uncle said.

He gave us a torch with the keys to go up and check the second floor.

"Be careful. We are not sure if all bulbs are fine. Lock it properly after seeing. We can-not climb up to check."

We nodded and took the keys. The lights were working and we didn't need the torch. As we climbed for the second floor, it was visible that it was not used for very long. The stairs had thick layer of dust, and long spider webs hanging from up. He was walking ahead. I was close behind, holding tight his shirt from behind. He opened the door and started the torch to locate the switch. We stepped in. It was a big living room, with a small kitchen on its side. Two bedrooms opened at one end of it, and a bathroom on the other. It was a bare house only with lights and fans. The floor had thick grey layer of dust. Big spider webs were there in every corner of the place. Cockroaches were playing freely everywhere.

"The house is too big for us, but fine. Let us check the rent." He said, adding, "Let us try to negotiate. We will take it till Rs 1200/. We are not getting anything else."

We locked and came down. He gave the keys and said, "House is too big. We don't have any furniture or anything to keep. Also, we both will be out from morning till late evening. But we will take it. Please do something on the rent part."

"I have already reduced a lot for you both. I cannot give for less than 1500/. Our son will not agree. And, cleaning etc you will have to take care. We will not be able to do."

We told them to give us ten minutes to talk and decide. We came out.

I said, "will we be able to manage the rent from Rs 900/ to Rs 1500/!"

"We are trying since a week. We are not getting anything in this too. We have to vacate the room in few days. We take this now. If we will not be able to manage, you go back. I will again stay with my friend."

This seemed to be the only option at that point. I nodded. We went in, gave them Rs 500/ and confirmed.

The next week went in cleaning and preparing the place to live. I would directly go there from work and clean for around an hour and come to our room. I would then cook dinner, wash clothes, take bath and keep things ready for the next day.

He would complain that I don't sleep. I just seem to faint as I lie down.

Two days went in just removing the hanging webs and killing the cockroaches, all the while saving myself from them climbing on my feet.

He wanted that I only clean one room and kitchen. "We can leave the other rooms closed. We don't need to clean the complete house."

"I can't live with cockroaches running in other room. We will have to sleep down. What if they will climb on us! I am scared. I will go only after cleaning fully."

After the success of mission cockroaches and webs it was easy work. Since the house had no furniture, I just washed the entire house. Now it was ready for us to move in.

On the Sunday morning, an auto took our suitcases, bags, cylinder, gas, bucket, brooms and us to our new house.

He went and brought a mattress from his friend. It was a single bed thin cotton mattress. It occupied our bedroom. The suitcases and bags went in the second room. The living room got a carton box as our table and a mat for us to sit. Kitchen was set quickly. I lit the gas, boiled the milk and spilled few drops of it with my finger.

He sat on the kitchen slab, singing my favourite songs as I prepared food. We enjoyed our first meal on our new table in our new house. We were happy that now we can live without the owner's 'this is not allowed here' look.

• • •

We both were set in the routine.

He would leave early and come late in the evening. We will take dinner and talk about the day. Then his friend will come. They both will study and do their assignments in the living room till midnight or at times more. He will then come and squeeze himself on our small mattress.

I will leave for work soon after him. I will go on the bike given to me by the company. After my work hours I will immediately rush, as I would have to pick vegetables daily. I will reach home and quickly cook the dinner. I will then clean the house, wash clothes and take bath. I had tied a rope on the side of the other room. I would dry the clothes there. After dinner as he would sit with his friend, I would go and sleep.

The monsoons had set in. Every evening there used to be heavy downpour, continuing almost for the whole night. There used be loud sound of water pouring on the roof and on the metal sheet parapet extending over the stairs. The first floor was vacant. Even our rooms on second floor were empty. This made the sound echo more on our floor. He would keep getting up in the night, checking the door and windows. I would not know any of this. He would tell me this the next day, with his everyday complaint, "you don't sleep. You seem to faint."

On the way was a wholesale market. We had no fridge to store anything. And we could not afford anything going bad. So, I would pick milk and vegetables only enough to last for a day. I was not used to drinking tea that time. And my salary was not enough for milk to fit in. I would take a small milk packet and mix some water in it. I will make it enough for a cup of tea for him and will also save some to set curd for both of us. He loved boondi raita and it gave me more levy to add water in the curd too.

Once during my daily vegetable shopping, I saw plums with a vendor. I picked one piece after thoroughly checking it. I negotiated hard to get it in the change I could manage. I kept it in the plate as we sat for dinner. He saw the plum and lost his cool.

"Plum! Are you crazy? We are not able to get milk to make tea properly and you want to eat plums!" he said adding angrily, "Ye baap ki ruyisi baap ke ghar karna. Kabhi badam, kadhi plums! Dal roti kha sakti ho toh raho or go back. Your husband doesn't have means for all these."

I too got angry. With tears flowing I said, "I bargained so hard to get it, thinking we can at least eat one in the season. But don't worry. I will eat less chapati two days and compensate for this. Now onwards I will not get anything. You only get everything and manage however you want to."

Crying loudly, I got up and went away. He came and held my hands. "I am sorry. Don't cry. I was just upset that we are struggling for basic things and you are spending on these. It's OK. You bring and eat if you want."

I didn't answer. I just could not. I just cried, and cried for very long. And he sat holding me tight.

Then we ate dinner, and also the plum, savouring each bit of bite.

The plum that night did taste very special. But, after that night plums never remained same for me. Till today he hears "plums taste better only at my 'baap ke ghar'."

I had also bought some almonds and kept. In the morning, I put one in his mouth. Surprised he said, "almonds also! Madam, do we have money for them!" Putting one in my mouth, I replied, "I am sure we can manage one each in your madam's rule." He smiled, hugged me tight and we left again for our long day.

• • •

By now I knew about most of the models and their specifications. The first target of the floor was for the bike given to me to commute. There were hardly any enquiries for it, probably since it was a gear bike and was not perceived comfortable by girls. I was the only female staff riding that bike. This gave me an edge and all the enquiries for it on phone or walk-ins were directed to me. I was enjoying the work and it was giving me free time too.

MD sir had a big collection of books in his office. He was generous to lend them to me to read. I would take a book every second day and spend all my free time in office reading them.

Soon, the target of the floor changed to a new bike launch. At first, it felt odd to suddenly prove a new bike as the best, over the one I was proving the best till the previous day. But a session as a shadow rep of the manager, and I was ready to handle this.

There were many enquiries and walk-ins for this new launch. They were given in order to all. The free time in between was used by me to complete the books I would pick from MD sir's office.

I had requested the manager not to give me an enquiry nearing my leaving time. Knowing that I stayed far and the rain was heavier in the evenings, he would give me an additional one during the day and let me go at my time.

One day I was sitting at my desk reading a book when the manager came up to me and said, "An enquiry is here for a bike. He is more comfortable in English. Could you please take him around."

I nodded, kept the book and went with him to the waiting area. He introduced me to the person and left. I greeted him and guided him to the display room of the showroom.

I showed him all the models of the bikes along with the features of each. I explained him the benefits of the new model. I even took permission from manager to take him to the service station as he wanted to start and check the bikes.

He was asking multiple questions about each model. For every feature I told, he had an additional question. He was polite and seemed to know everything about each bike. I was answering and explaining patiently, all the time wondering why is he asking me when he knows all.

He spent couple of hours checking the entire showroom. He then wanted to check through the brochures to compare the features. I took him to my desk and gave him the brochures.

As a protocol for prospective buyers, I got coffee and snacks arranged for him.

While flipping the pages of the brochure he asked, "just out of curiosity, by any chance are you a management graduate?"

I looked at him and said, "Yes. But what makes you think that!"

"Marketing major? Yes?", without answering he asked again.

I nodded.

"I am pursuing my management degree right now. So, I am kind of your junior. The hours today were like an internship for me Ms senior. All we learn in theory, I was relating to it completely all this time."

I smiled and said, "thank you. From which institute are you pursuing your MBA."

He said that he was in his second year of the management degree program in USA and was here for his holidays.

I could not stop myself and said in a lower voice, "I know I should be encouraging you to buy a bike. But if you are here only for the holidays, I would suggest don't buy such an expensive bike! Why you want to waste so much money if you have to go in a month's time."

He smiled, sipped his coffee and said, "You will then lose your sale and commission."

Thinking that I should have not given the suggestion, I said, "True. It's a good bike. If you do want to buy, do buy it from our showroom only. I will try with the manager to get you some additional accessories in the bike."

I then took him to the manager and excused myself, as I had already crossed my time to rush home.

That night during dinner as we were talking about our day, I told my husband about that walk-in.

After listening he said, "tomorrow he will ask to take you out for coffee or dinner."

Nervous and upset, I collected the dishes and got up. Banging them more than washing, I said, ""Just like that! You just say anything without thinking. He has come there to buy a bike. And what you think he wouldn't have seen my marriage bangles or my mangalsutra!"

Sitting on the kitchen slab and swinging his legs, he said, "you write and keep it. He will come tomorrow and ask you. Your bangles and mangalsutra can pass as accessories."

I was quiet. I was worried. I was scared.

"OK. If for a minute we think he will tell this, what will I do?" I asked, nervously.

"What will you tell! If you want to go say Yes! He is doing MBA in USA and is buying a bike to enjoy his vacations. Ameer baap ka beta hai! Go! Enjoy coffee or dinner!

"Shut up. Just tell what will I do? I will not go tomorrow," I said, feeling nervous.

"Daffu! He will come again if you will not go tomorrow. Just tell him that you are married and you can't go with him!"

I was repeatedly telling myself that this situation won't come. But I was also repeatedly preparing myself not to get nervous.

Next day I reached office as usual in time. But I was anxious. I asked the manager if he confirmed to buy the previous evening. Manager said that he wanted some time to think.

I was hoping that he would have taken my suggestion and dropped the idea to buy the bike.

I was on the display floor with another walk-in.

The manager came and said, "He has come. He has some more queries before he decides. He wants to understand them from you."

"I have explained everything I knew. Can you please handle now. I might not know more. And I am with this walk-in right now."

"I told him you are busy. But he said he will wait. You finish this and go. Call me if you are not able to address any query. Try that we close it today. See if some discount will help."

I was quiet. I tried to go slow with the enquiry I was handling. All through I was hoping that he might not wait for long, and will either leave or agree to go with another staff.

After finishing I came to the waiting area. He was still there. I greeted him and said, "sir told you are waiting for me with some more queries. Sorry, it got late with another enquiry. But sir would have addressed your queries better."

"I can wait longer. You might be tired. You take some time," he said.

"It's OK. I am fine. Please tell me," I asked.

"I have decided to go against your suggestion. I will buy the bike. But before finalizing I wanted to check it one more time. Since you helped me decide on it, I would prefer you help me finalize it too."

"Sure. Please come."

I took him again to the display section. He kept asking random questions about the bike. He checked it again and said, "I will go for it."

"Thank you. You will have to complete some documentation work. Please come. I will inform sir."

I called the manager. He came to my desk and explained the process. "Please get him some coffee. I will send the forms here to fill."

He was sitting and having coffee. I was filling the details in the forms.

"I am very happy that I got the bike I wanted. It's lunch time. I am hungry. Would you mind joining me for a quick lunch break."

My heart beat increased. Without looking up I said, "sorry. I can't leave during my working hours. You please carry on. I will keep these documents ready."

"What about coffee after your work hours? I hope you are allowed that?"

I looked at him and said, "I need to rush home after work. I won't be able to join."

"OK. Then on the weekends? Now don't give an excuse. Whatever time suits you, we can go at that time. The bike needs a celebration."

I was getting nervous and knew that it was reflecting on my face. I tried hard to keep my voice flat.

"I am really sorry. Weekdays are very busy. So, I like to spend time with my husband on weekends. But I will check with him. If he is fine, we both will surely join your bike celebration."

He was now quiet. It was clear from the look on his face that he was upset with my reply. He moved back on the chair. I looked down and continued filling the forms.

I then called the manager and gave the forms to him. He took him for further process about the accessories and payment.

I was worried that he might again come with something. So, I immediately got up and went to another staff's desk. I tried to engage myself talking to her, waiting for him to leave.

He came there and said, "Thank you. I will come tomorrow to take the delivery. Bye."

"Bye", I said.

• • •

Next day there was a day-long meeting and an ideation session for the upcoming National Dealer's Meet. Before leaving that day, I went to MD sir and requested him to allow me to join the meeting.

He said, "You are very new. Do you think you are ready with ideas to bring some difference here and at higher level?"

"Very much sir. I am confident that the team will surely see value in my inputs on. Please allow me a chance."

He smiled and nodded. "See you tomorrow. Come prepared."

I was very happy. More than getting the opportunity to share my ideas, it was about avoiding to be in some uncomfortable situation again next day.

When I reached home, my husband was already there.

"What happened?" he asked.

I told him all.

"I am not coming anywhere! Why did you say that we both will join! You could have just told that you are not interested and closed it. What if he will come tomorrow and invite both of us! I am just not coming", he shouted.

"That would have been rude. He could be genuine. And what's the harm in both of us going together!" I told angrily.

"I will just not come. You can go if you want to," he said.

"Anyways no one is going. Don't worry. I have managed to be in full day session tomorrow so that I don't have to handle anything of this if he comes tomorrow," I said, going in the kitchen to cook.

His friend came and they sat with their work.

I also finished the house work and sat for long, thinking and preparing notes for the challenge I had randomly taken upon myself. Occasionally I would drift away, wondering if the way I perceived and handled it was flawed or correct! But then I would drag myself to prepare for the new challenge.

Next day I reached ready with my detailed notes. The meeting was in the open space in front of MD sir's office on the first floor. The waiting area and working desks on the ground floor were visible from up. The meeting began with the briefing by MD sir followed by the discussion about ways to enhance differentiation within and in the upcoming dealer's meet. After everyone shared, all eyes turned to me. I started sharing the points I had made. I had made them based on the interactions and inputs I had gathered during my handling of enquiries and walk-ins. They were all taken by the team. I was asked to discuss with the manager and come up with inputs to execute them.

As this discussion was going on, I noticed him sitting down in the waiting area. I avoided looking there and continued.

"Sir. I am not sure if this input will bring much value, but I suggest we should implement uniform for the staff. Right now there is a significant difference in our dressing. It impacts how a walk-in perceives a staff. Uniform attire will help build a similar first impression and our place will look professional."

As everyone started sharing their inputs on this, I stood with my fingers crossed.

I was not sure if it was practically possible for them to spend on getting dresses for all. But I had to propose this due to the situation I was in. With only four dresses appropriate for work, and no possibility to buy more, this was my only saviour if accepted.

"It is good. We can start by implementing this with the female staff. You join me in my office after lunch. I will brief on how we will move ahead on this," MD sir said.

"Sure sir. Thank you so much," I replied beaming happily.

As we were breaking for lunch, a staff came and told that he is waiting and wants to talk to me. I told to tell him that I am in a meeting till evening and won't be able to meet in between.

After quick lunch I joined MD sir. The manager was also there. Sir told, that he has asked his daughter to come to office the next day. I should take her to the market on the bike. She will select the dresses for staff. She will then send the tailor to take measurements to stitch the dresses.

"And one more thing. We want you to give the presentation in the dealer's meet," he added.

"Sir, I have not even completed a month. I am very new to this industry. I might not be able to answer if they will ask questions about this company or this industry." I replied nervously.

"We have one week. The manager will help you with all the information. From tomorrow you be on this floor. You will get the computer. Make the presentation. I am sure you can do it well," he said, adding "We should get the best dealer award this year too."

I nodded and came out.

The manager gave me some files to read. He opened the previous year's presentation and asked me to check that too.

That night I was very happy. I told my husband that I took the approval for uniform for work.

"It might take two-three weeks for you to get them. My course will complete in another couple of months. We will have to move where I get my job. What will you do with them?" he asked.

"We don't know how long it will take for you to get a job. Also, you might get it in this city only. I am happy that for now my issue is solved," I said while preparing dinner.

"What about the other issue? Did he come and meet you again today?" he asked.

"That issue is also solved, I think. He came. I didn't meet him," I replied.

I was thinking and hoping that he will not come now.

Next week was very busy at work with collecting data, making notes, working on the presentation and reviewing with sir.

In between sir's daughter came and we went to a shop in the market. She asked to show the materials for dresses. I suggested to take something which will not wrinkle and dry faster, to be useful in monsoons and not require ironing. We selected two prints. She asked him to send the tailor to take measurements for the staff.

"We will try to implement this new thing in the new month. Please get it done on priority" I requested the shopkeeper.

He nodded.

We came back, all the way talking about each other's college, subjects, city etc. She asked me to meet again.

I smiled and said, "sure. I am in your showroom every day. Any time you can come."

She shook her head and laughed, "good. I will."

• • •

It was the time of peak monsoons. It was a routine to rain from late afternoon till the early morning hours. My husband used to take the umbrella so I had his raincoat. Most of the days I had to ride back home in heavy rain. The traffic would be heavy and slow. I would just pick something which the couple of vendors at the entry of vegetable market had and would rush home. The raincoat helped little and I will reach home almost soaked.

On the way back I had to cross an underpass. It used to be like a mini river every time it rained. A train would pass over it around the same time. To me it seemed a very long and slow train. First day when I encountered it, I saw everyone waiting for the train to cross. I also stopped. The train just didn't seem to move, and I just could not keep waiting.

I started my bike and rushed. Everyone started screaming, asking me to wait. But I just couldn't afford to wait and just went.

This would happen every time the rain, the train and my time matched.

• • •

On the weekend I reached very early. I had to go with the manager for the dealer's meet. I was nervous. I checked the presentation once and we left.

The hall was full with the teams from the entire zone. The teams started presenting as per their turn. Then it was our turn. I presented and explained our numbers with different models over the entire year. I compared it with the data presented by the teams before me to show that we did better not only overall but even in the months when others didn't.

Then was the question hour. After many questions around numbers and approach, someone from audience asked, "being a new employee in the company how genuinely and honestly you believe and know it to be the best organisation?" I replied, "The answer is in your question only. Each company here would surely have new employees. But none could trust any of them with the opportunity to be here today? Every team I interacted with here have been a regular at this meet. It is only at my company, that an employee who has just completed a month has been given an opportunity to represent it at this prestigious event."

And the roaring applause and award both were ours.

On Monday MD sir called me to his office. He said, "it was fantastic. You did great. Your celebration dinner is on us. You give the bill in accounts and they will give you Rs 500/. Go and enjoy."

I was very happy. I rushed home. Breathless with excitement, I told him about it.

He was also happy. He said, "Great! You take the money from them. We will not go out to eat. It will help to manage through the month."

I didn't like it.

I said, "You told me to tell that it is just to keep me busy and get some pocket money. Now how can I tell them that you are not working and I need the money to manage things? I will have to tell that you are doing a course and we might be here for some time only. In this case I might lose the job!"

"You don't need to tell all this. They are anyway giving this money to you. You just talk to the accountant and tell that you lost the bill. Why they will bother about the bill!" he said.

I said, "I am not doing all this. If he will tell me to take permission from MD sir, I will tell him the correct thing. It's fine. We will not go. But I can't do all this."

"Then take me for a good dinner. Why should we let it go waste," he said, hugging me tight.

"Yay! We will go to the restaurant opposite to the lake," I said hugging him back.

"We might not get dinner in this money in that restaurant. Chai Pani pila ke wapas le aayegi tu," he said laughing.

"We will eat little. But let us go there. Candle light mein paani ke saath papad toh kha hi lenge!" I said.

Next day we got ready and reached the restaurant we would see every Sunday sitting near the lake side. We went inside. We were guided to a table. As we settled, water and papad was served with the menu card. We both started laughing.

"Candle light main pani aur papad toh ho gaya! Now shall we leave?" he asked smiling.

I took the menu and calculated things which could fit in Rs 500/. I said, "We can get a soup, dal and rotis. Papad is our starter. So we have soup, starter and main course. For dessert we will get a scoop of ice cream. I am sure I will be able to get additional Rs 50/ approved. So, we get to have a full three course meal."

"What if they will not approve?", he asked.

"They surely should. Now leave them and let us enjoy," I replied.

We spent a lot of time there, enjoying our first dinner date after marriage. We then drove around the lanes on the bike, he singing my favourite songs and I resting on his back.

We started the routine of the week again the next day.

I was hesitant to approach sir for approval. But when I went to return the book to his office, I told him about the bill exceeding Rs 50/.

He said, "500 should have been enough. But its fine for this time. You give it to the accountant and ask him to call me."

I was relieved and happy. Full week I handled more enquiries and work for the special consideration extended to me.

• • •

The next couple of weeks seemed to balance the joyride I was sailing in.

Twice a week I had to give the bike at the service station. It was checked, serviced, refuelled and kept ready for me to pick in the evening. The service station was right behind the showroom. The ground floor was the vehicle inspection area. The approach to the service area was through a small ramp which turned into a steep slope. Normally a person would be there and I would handover the bike to him. That day there was no one there. I was not sure of leaving the bike down. I decided to take it up. I crossed the ramp and turned to the slope. I was almost till the top that the bike suddenly stalled and started rolling down the slope. I wanted to apply the break, but my feet were busy trying to control the rolling bike from skidding. In an instant the bike rammed into the wall behind the slope. I felt a hard blow and the bike was on me.

The bang brought everyone at the service station there. Someone removed the bike. Someone helped me get up. Someone gave me water.

"Are you fine?" the service station in-charge asked, adding "You don't have to bring the bike up. You should leave it down".

I had pain in my elbow and feet. My heart was pounding. I was scared and worried about the bike. I said, "I am very sorry. Please check if the bike is not damaged."

"Only the back light seems to be damaged. We will fix it. You seem to be hurt. We will get an auto for you. You go home," he said.

I was very worried. I didn't want to take leave. I said I will be fine and went to the show room.

He brought the bike after lunch and parked it outside the showroom. He said, "Bike is fine. Now onwards you park it here only. We will pick from here for checking and servicing."

I thanked him. I was relieved that both me and bike didn't hurt more. Bike got immediately repaired. My pain took over a week.

Our new uniforms had come. This had removed my big everyday stress.

One evening as I stepped out to leave, it had already started drizzling. I had to pick my husband from his friend's place as they were preparing together for some test. I was hoping to reach before the rain got heavy.

I started the bike. I had just taken the bike down on the road that something came and dashed me. Next I knew was people holding and taking me inside the showroom. I was made to sit on the sofa. I took some water. My toe and hand from elbow down were bruised and bleeding little. My colleagues gave me first aid.

I was worried and asked them to check the bike. They said it seems fine. Due to dashing, it skidded and fell on me so I got bruised more.

They asked me to take an auto home as I was hurt. I was worried about the auto money to go home and again to come the next morning. I told them that I was fine to drive and go.

The news of my accident reached my husband before me. Since I got late, he had called the showroom. They informed him about the accident and the delay.

As I entered, he and his friend were waiting with their strings of questions.

"Are you fine?" "Why did you ride and come?" "Why can't you ride slowly and carefully?" "Kabhi wall, kabhi auto, kahan kahan bhid jaati hai!"

"I don't know what happened," I said walking with a limp. When I checked, my knee and leg was also bruised. He put medicine and bandage. We took dinner there and came home.

By morning the pain had increased and I had fever. I asked him to inform my manager. It took two days for the fever and pain to subside. For over 10 days I was limping at work, and finding it hard to climb up and down the stairs at home. But, steadily recovered.

• • •

The next month was usual routine for me but hectic for him. Companies had started coming to the institute for recruitment. His friend got the offer first. We celebrated it in our house.

He was very stressed for missing in the first round. He was waiting anxiously. In the next round he got the offer. We were very happy.

He had to go to collect the offer letter from the company's office. We both went on the bike. I was waiting outside as he went inside. After sometime he came running out, excited. "I did it! I got it! Guess how much I will get," he asked holding my hands. I was super happy. I said, "double!". "Three times", he excitedly said waving his offer envelope.

As we reached back home, he hugged me and started crying. He then held my hands and said, "I don't know how you managed all this. But now you will never have to put through anything like this. I will only always manage everything." Now I was also crying.

And till today I am happily helping him keep his promise!

• • •

The offer letter had the preferred joining in another city within two weeks. He said that he will ask for a later joining. "We can go home and spend some time there before moving to a new city," he said.

"Let's not delay it. What if they will then ask you to wait! It will be difficult to manage. You go and join. I will go home and join you with the things we will need there," I said.

He too didn't want to risk his starting and confirmed his joining.

Next day he joined me to go and talk to MD sir. He told sir about his offer and relocation and I requested him to relieve me. He said that he would surely not want to relieve me. But he understands that I would have to go.

He gave me the number of the MD of the company showroom in the city we were moving. He said, "Go and meet him if you want to work. I will talk to him. We would love to have you continue in our company. And, come over for dinner on the weekend. My daughter would not be happy if you will leave without meeting her."

I was sad that I will have to leave the people with whom I had made such loving bond. And I was blessed to have them in my life in those uncertain times.

• • •

I left for home. He went and joined his new job in a new city. In two weeks, he took one bedroom house and I joined him there. Ten days after was Diwali. Since he had just joined, we could not go home for Diwali. He told his parents to come for Diwali. But they refused. My parents came over to be with us on our first Diwali.

Some things I had brought with me. Some my parents brought along. Some came through the packers. It had been only two weeks in the house, and only a couple of days that the luggage had arrived. He came from office in the evening and gave us a breaking news. He was selected to be put on a project, and he will have to move to the project location in a week's time.

I had just started thinking of settling with him, and again it seemed to be snapped. I suggested he goes for the project and I stay here. "All the stuff has moved here. I can join the company showroom while trying for some other jobs."

His project was for around a year. He and my parents didn't want me to be alone so far from home. It was decided that he will go for the project. My parents will help me wind up and transport the stuff back to home again.

And, I will again go back home with them.

We started packing everything in the same boxes we had unpacked just a couple of days before.

That evening he went with dad to get somethings from the neighbourhood market. After sometime they both entered, dad supporting and holding him. His foot had swelling and he was having pain in his leg. As he was turning the bike, it fell on his leg. We took an auto and took him to a nearby clinic. He had got his ankle fractured.

In a couple of days, a big cast was put on his leg. He was very worried and stressed that he might lose the opportunity to be on the project. I said, "Tell them that you are fine and can manage. If you can manage with your cast, why will they go into the hassle of preparing a replacement. It could be little difficult, but you will be able to work with it."

He left for his project with a cast on his leg and a stick in his hand.

After he left, we wrapped up everything, sent the bike and luggage and handed over the house. Before the month could complete, I was again on the fifty-two hours long journey, back with my parents.

His project was in a heavy chemicals factory. The factory was around sixteen kilometers away from the nearest town. Near the factory was a colony for the managers and staff of the factory. He was staying in a guest house in the colony, along with his other teammates.

He said that he can't call me there as family is not allowed to stay in the guest house.

I was at my in-laws' place. Around a month went away and he could not workout anything to call me there. Dad was now upset. He said, "You can't stay in guest house. But he can take a room in the city. Something has to be worked out. After this he will get some other project in some other place. Will he keep doing this! Tell him I am coming to drop you. Let him take a room or book in a hotel. But you are coming."

I told him this.

He refused. He said, "the town is very small. To find a proper place to live would be difficult. Also, to work out the commute to the factory would be harder. I am busy from early morning till evening. You will be bored as there is nothing to do and engage here. Why don't you take up some job there to keep yourself busy. Once something works out, you can join here."

I refused. I said, "It has been enough of leaving my jobs. If I will now take a job, I will not leave it at all. Then where ever your project comes, or where ever you go, I will not come there."

"You think I am not trying or I don't want to have you here!"

"Then take a room in a hotel or anywhere else. I am coming."

I packed up some basic stuff. Dad again started with me. He came till the main city station to take me. Dad took the immediate return train for another over twenty-three hours journey.

We took the overnight train and reached to the taluk. He had booked a room in a hotel there. He immediately got ready and left for factory. He told that there is a dhaba near the hotel. I can bring food from there.

I freshened up. Went and got food from the dhaba, ate and slept off. I spent the afternoon reading in the room. He came in the evening. We went around the town, ate dinner at the same dhaba and came back.

Next day I went around exploring the place. The place was dusty but the weather was pleasant. The hotel was in the middle of a busy market. There was a dhaba, couple of small food joints, a small restaurant, some grocery and vegetable stores and a small gift shop. I saw a small computer training place amidst these shops. I went inside and took details about the various courses and trainings they offered there.

I would spend some time reading and writing in the room, some time checking out the shops around. In the night when he would come, I will tell him about the various things I would have checked and found about the neighbourhood.

We were there for a week. One evening when he came back, he said that his site manager has offered a room on the terrace of the guest house. It has some extra stuff of the guest house and they will not remove it. We can check if we want to take it and live there.

I was excited to go there. I told him to take it. I said that if it has a bed and a bathroom, we can surely manage. He will not have the hassle to commute, and I will also not have to be closed in a hotel room whole day.

And we took our suitcases and moved to the guest house.

• • •

The team members of the project were given rooms to stay in the guest house. It had a cook. The team, the visitors and all guests took all meals here. The team was given a car to commute from guest house to factory. They would leave after breakfast, come for lunch and would be back again in the evening for dinner

The room given to us had a double bed in the middle. All around it was the stock for the guest room. There were mattresses, pillows, bedsheets, toiletries, cereals, spices, electrical items and much more.

He asked, "are you sure to live here?"

I said, "We will only have to sleep here. Full day you will be out. I will also try to find something to stay out of the room. And I will clean and set these things so that it doesn't look like a store."

"It is a store room. And don't take out your cleaning ginnie unnecessarily here," he said.

Next day as he went to work, I took the stuff to clean and dust from the staff. I sorted all the stuff and set them on one side of the room. I scrubbed cleaned the room and bathroom. The room now had everything stacked and kept neatly on one side. If you keep your back to that side, the room now was a small clean room. I kept the door open full day to reduce the mix of smells of spices, old fabrics and dampness.

I was happy. He was surprised.

There were two cooks in the guest house. I offered to help them in the kitchen. They refused that I am a guest and should rest and enjoy. But I would go and stand in the kitchen while they worked. One of them was from army. He shared lot of stories from his days moving around with soldiers, cooking for them and how they would manage where supplies were hard to reach.

I would now help them for some time after breakfast in kitchen. At times they allowed me to cook lunch for all. And everyone did enjoy it.

They would ask if I want to eat something specific or something to be cooked differently. I told them, "everything is fine, only my rotis I like extra roasted."

And every time they served rotis after that, they brought two extra-roasted rotis separately for me. And the whole team would tease them for being partial to the lady in the room.

• • •

It was a small beautiful colony. It had bungalows for the managers of the factory. All had beautifully maintained gardens. There was also a small park, a community centre and a school for the children of the factory staff inside. On one side of the colony were staff quarters for the teachers of the school.

After a couple of days of settling, I went to the school. I told in the office that I am looking for job and want to meet the principal. The person sent me to meet the president. He said, "You are our guest, and are here for a short duration. It would not work to have you join for a short period."

I said, "I can come as a volunteer and help, if that would be possible."

He replied, "You are young. Enjoy your stay here. Today evening you come and meet my wife. She will surely take you in the ladies' club. You will get to do and enjoy a lot with them."

I nodded with a smile. I walked out sad.

But, at that moment I didn't realise that I was going to meet a bunch of beautifully loving and lively ladies, leaving whom will make me sad and cry.

In the evening I went to his house. He was sitting with his wife in their garden. I greeted them and sat. He introduced me to her, "by her credentials this young girl seems to be very hardworking. She wants to do something during her short stay here too. You can see if she can join the ladies club."

He then excused himself. She started talking to me. I shared details about my background and about my stay there. She said, "Our club has all ladies much older than you. But we do take up lot of different activities. We have our meeting after two days. You come for it. Everyone can meet you. And you will also get to know more. If all goes well, you will be our new member."

I went for the meeting. And all did go very well. I became their new member.

They would organize activities every week. These ranged from vegetable carving to stitching to writing to painting to singing and more. Then there were morning and evening walks loaded with laughter, often followed by meditation.

I was enjoying, always preparing and working on something. And he was complaining that I was always busy.

It had been a couple of weeks that I had joined the ladies club. One evening when he came back from the factory he told that the vice president had called him and offered a house for us to stay in the staff quarters. The ladies' club had raised it up to provide a proper place to us to stay.

He was very happy. I was too touched by this caring gesture.

I went to thank them the next day. I was too emotional. They hugged me and said, "don't worry. We wanted one more place to stop by for tea and snacks. And we don't want to do it in the store room of the guest house. Go set up your house. We might stop by any day after the walk."

• • •

We picked up our stuff and moved to our new place. It was a two bedroom house on the first floor of one of the staff quarters buildings. It didn't require much effort to clean and set. It had a double bed and gas. I had brought the basic things with me. We were immediately settled.

The car will pass through our building to pick and drop him. Once he would leave after breakfast, I would clean the house, wash clothes and prepare lunch. As he left after lunch, I would also get ready and leave.

I had joined a computer course in the institute near the hotel I stayed for a week. I had opted for the late afternoon batch as I was free during that time. I would take the afternoon bus from outside the colony. It took around one hour to reach. I would always use it to take a nap in that time.

The class was usually for one hour – one day class, one day practice time. They agreed to allow me two hours. So, I would commute alternate days instead of coming every day. At times I would also pick up the groceries and vegetables if I had some time in between finishing my class and the return bus.

In the next building of the staff quarters lived the art teacher who taught at school. In the evenings he took art classes at his house. Two days I would go there to learn oil on canvas. I learnt some real good techniques and made some pieces which I dearly adore even today.

With these, and with the activities at ladies' club my schedule was super packed during the week days.

There was a walkway from behind the colony that led to the beach side. Every Saturday morning, we would walk there and spend time on the beach side. The taluk was a site of a sacred Jyotirlinga. Every Saturday evening the entire team would go there. We all would spend the entire evening there, and would return after enjoying the sunset over the waves on its sea shore.

Saturday also had another regular ritual. After dinner, we both will play the game of scrabble with crazy challenges for the loser. I borrowed a dictionary from the school library through a teacher. Every Friday I would check out new words from each letter to be able to beat him in the game on Saturday. And many a times I did succeed! And he always readily accepted my challenges. Though, I would always crib about the challenges he gave.

How the ten months passed and the project got completed, we didn't realise. It was an emotional farewell with my loving ladies club gang.

The vice president sir invited us for the farewell dinner to his house. He said to him, "this dinner is not for you as the project team member. It is for you as the husband of your wife." He said, "I fully know. As any husband, I am always behind my wife." Everyone had a good laugh.

We enjoyed the evening before we left the place. A small place nestled far and away, overflowing with genuine love and care.

• • •

We went to our native from there. After spending a week at home, he went to the base city of his company. I was again at my in laws place for a month. He again took a house on a rent. My parents again came to drop me.

The trains ran twice a week between my native and his base location. And the journey was over fifty hours long. Due to their office schedules and my siblings' exams, they could not stay till the next available train schedule. So, they dropped me till the nearest city and took the return train the same day. But their already double travel time shot by over ten hours due to a derailment incident on the tracks.

In around one and a half years that we were now married, this shuttling had kind of become a routine. I was now upset about my parent's repeated travel due to me. My in laws didn't want to travel for me. And my parents and he won't want me to travel alone.

I told him that I would now stay there itself even if he needs to travel. Or we will go and come together.

But what you want, life doesn't give you just like it.

In the years that followed they would always come to be with me whenever his travel schedule was longer. The train attenders now knew them well and they knew most of them by their names. They had become our guides about which attender will help more, what to take at which station to eat and where to be alert of what.

It had been a couple of weeks that we had again settled in a new house in the city. An extremely pleasant surprise came our way. Why a surprise, sure is a separate chapter. We were super joyous, and at top of the world. A new member was coming in our family.

In a few days, I was super sick. I would sleep the entire twenty-four hours. The only moments I would get up would be just to throw up. I was super dizzy all the time, finding it hard to walk or even open my eyes. I was not able to take anything and was in and out of emergency.

In a week, he panicked.

My mother told him that I would be like this for some months. His mother said, "I would not know how to handle this. You ask her mom to come."

My mom was in service and had just reached back. It was decided that she will come for two weeks and his mom will come for two weeks. Based on my condition, they would decide further.

My mom came. She would make various things, trying that if I could hold them for some time before throwing up.

• • •

It had been a week that my mom was here. One evening he came and excitedly informed that he has been selected for a three months on-site project abroad.

I was in no state to react strongly to it. But I told him that I will go along with him.

He said that family is not allowed to travel along as it is a very short-term project. And that it was for this opportunity that he had risked everything. He might not get this opportunity soon, and he just doesn't want to miss it.

I was not in the state of health to insist on staying back alone. I stayed quiet.

He had to travel in two weeks. His mom was coming after a week. It was decided that I will go with her to our native again, and he will go ahead with his travel.

My mom left and his mom arrived. He alone did my packing and also his. Since it was a three months project, we did not vacate the house.

I just know that I completed the long journey in sleep mode.

He left a couple of days after we left.

I stayed in the same shaky and sleepy mode for around another month. Slowly after that I was getting better to hold myself up again on my legs.

A whole lot happened around me during the next two months I was there. But I was dearly holding on to, and living the blessing breathing inside me.

He returned after three months and we came back to our house. The next few months amused us with a new experience and a new emotion every day. We were enjoying every bit of that journey.

Some moments stay forever etched in our hearts. The moment we held our doll in our embrace remains one of those precious moments. My parents being with us in that very moment filled it with immense blessings and joy it brought in our lives.

Connect. Share

Every moment leaves something behind.

Some become memories we cherish, some become lessons we carry, and some quietly touch our hearts.

If these moments made you pause, feel, think or connect even a little, then these moments have found a home in your heart.

And, if somewhere these moments have nudged your heart to share your moments - feel free to connect at **lettersforkirti@gmail.com**

Perhaps, another unforgettable memoir of our moments is already waiting to begin.

www.ingramcontent.com/pod-product-compliance
Lightning Source LLC
LaVergne TN
LVHW100333210926
848480LV00003B/1328
9798904794095